M000289493

To my friend and one of the best men I've had the honor of knowing!

your manic campaign manager & friend for the ages,

Remson

HOW TO SUCCEED IN POLITICS

(and Other Forms of Devil Worship)

Remso W. Martinez

How to Succeed in Politics (and Other Forms of Devil Worship)

Copyright © 2019 by Remso W. Martinez.

All Rights Reserved.

ISBN 978-1-64669-391-7

All rights reserved. No part of this book may be reproduced in any form or by any electronic or mechanical means including information storage and retrieval systems, without permission in writing from the author. The only exception is by a reviewer, who may quote short excerpts in a review.

Cover designed by 99designs

This book is a work of fiction. Names, characters, places, and incidents either are products of the author's imagination or are used fictitiously. Any resemblance to actual persons, living or dead, events, or locales is entirely coincidental.

Remso W. Martinez
Visit my website at rwmartinez.com

Printed in the United States of America

First Printing: Aug 2019
Kindle Direct Publishing

CONTENTS

Praise for *How to Succeed in Politics (and Other Forms of Devil Worship)*

"Remso Martinez astutely observes the ways in which the quest for political power not only attracts bad people, but also tempts good people to do bad things."

-LOGAN ALBRIGHT,
FREE THE PEOPLE

"Martinez is beautifully sardonic and disturbingly accurate in his depiction of the adventures of campaign worker Art Brown. The story's antihero is intelligent, hilarious and most importantly, honest. If you ever wanted to get inside the political process but were afraid the truth would cause you to want to commit ritualistic suicide, this book will guide you through while allowing you to keep your sanity.

-JEREMY CLIMER,
THE LAUNCH PAD MEDIA

"Remso is one of few authors who continues to make me laugh at modern America's political landscape. His excellent storytelling with a twinge of cynicism is just what this country needs. Remso's writing is only getting better, and more Hunter Thompson-esque, as time goes on. This book is sure to make readers laugh and think."

-TIM PREUSS,
THE TIM PREUSS PODCAST

"Politics is a blood sport, of that there is no question. Politicians and the political class will use you to further their political career, but not your issues. Remso lays this out in a hilarious and fun to read book. If you are interested in politics, or perhaps thinking of joining a political campaign, this is a must read."

-S. CHRIS ANDERS,
ACTON ADVOCACY GROUP

AUTHOR'S NOTE

This is a work of historical fiction. Although its form is that of an autobiography, it is not one. Space and time have been rearranged to suit the convenience of the book, and with the exception of public figures, any resemblance to persons living or dead is coincidental. The opinions expressed are those of the characters and should not be confused with the author's. Much research and detail has gone into providing an accurate portrayal of the real life public figures and individuals included in this book, such as descriptions, conversations, and events.

ACT I

"Unpopular opinion: I don't think I've ever called a politician a motherfucker, but I feel like it's particularly American to have that right."

~MATT KIBBE, WRITER, ECONOMIST, BEER ENTHUSIAST

CHAPTER 1

American Nightmare

Robert "Bobby" F. Kennedy was the Steve McQueen of politics, and anyone with two brain cells knows that. The sky is blue, the grass is green; disagree with any of that publicly and people will look at you funny. Bobby Kennedy had a look to him. People today still look at politicians using certain mannerisms and gestures and will say that they are "Kennedy-like." There are very few figures throughout American history who we can say are genuinely loved by the people regardless of color, creed, or political stripes. You'd have to go back to the Founding Fathers to find politicians who would be considered likable by today's standards. Bobby Kennedy was different. We remember him less for his specific policies and accomplishments, and more for how he made us feel. Bobby makes people feel proud to be American. I often wonder if we'd have the same thoughts about him if he hadn't been shot in public for the world to see.

I'm a cruel, stone-hearted rationalist, and I try not to let my emotions cloud my judgment, but by God, I've never voted Democrat in my life, and I would have worked for Bobby Kennedy for free if I were alive in 1968. He embodied the best of American potential, as he pointed us to look at the challenges of our past and the promises of our future. Bobby, much like his brother, the late President John F. Kennedy, is so universally loved amongst the American public that even conservative Republicans praise him. When Dan Quayle was tapped to be George H.W. Bush's vice-presidential pick in 1988, he often compared himself to JFK in public. It is so remarkably rare to reach that level of fame, a level which makes people ignore your faults and give you essentially blanket forgiveness of your sins. I think John may have been a cool guy, but a saint he was not. Bobby, however, was as straight as you could get having come from a family of bootleggers that discovered it was more profitable to transition to the world of legalized, organized crime, known as politics. Notice how we never discuss the bastard black sheep, Ted Kennedy, who lacked sincerity, the "cool" factor, and is best known through jokes about leaving blondes at the bottom of a lake.

We typically identify our heroes by those they opposed, which in Bobby's case means his feud with his brother's successor, the large-and-in-charge Texan, Lyndon B. Johnson, and the stuttering sadist and FBI Director, J. Edgar Hoover. Kennedy's firm opposition to the Vietnam war would also make him a standout figure in an era where war opposition was a political death sentence. In a time of severe distrust and disillusionment with every institute, every church, and everything tied with the American experience, Bobby was a shining example of American potential to many people.

Where there are heroes, however, there are also villains. While Bobby was combating state-sponsored segregation, racism, hatred, and the politics of rage, there was someone else who would later go down as the American Darth Vader; someone so despised their very name makes people cringe, small animals flee, and children cry. When American historians and political commentators think of a political figure who is universally despised, the consensus usually falls on someone who was as much of the opposite of Bobby Kennedy you could get- the walking, talking, slick-suited pitbull from Alabama, Governor George C. Wallace.

Go on Google and search quotes by Bobby Kennedy, and one of the top results you'll find is "the purpose of life is to contribute in some way to making things better." That is a nice quote to print out and put on your cubicle wall so you can stare at it when you're depressed at work. Instead, you see that nice and fluffy quote and you think "just stick it out, just stick out and you'll be home soon." It makes you feel good, and maybe you'll go and use it the next time you're in a conversation about a related topic of charity and compassion and want to seem virtuous. Now Google quotes from Wallace and see if there are any you want to stick up at your desk for the whole world to see. The first one I found was "I draw the line in the dust and toss the gauntlet before the feet of tyranny, and I say segregation now, segregation tomorrow, segregation forever." I doubt very much you are ever going to drop that into a water cooler conversation.

History remembers influential people less for their whole life's story, but for a few moments in time where they immensely impacted the lives of many. For many Americans, the image of Bobby standing on the back of a pickup truck in Indianapolis, telling a crowd of predominantly black Americans that Dr. Martin Luther King had been assassinated by a white man, stands out as one of the most memorable moments from the civil rights era. Bobby was able to command the respect of the crowd as he spoke from his personal experience of loss, telling the crowd how he too knew the feeling of losing a family member to a gunman. Bobby spoke to the crowd without bringing a large posse or crowd of press, and he did it on the turf of the people to whom MLK was attempting to bring justice. While rioting occurred throughout the country in many inner-city, black neighborhoods, Indianapolis was quiet and no rioting occurred thanks to Bobby's intervention and compassion. Moments like that make him the

Apostle Paul in the church of latter-day liberalism, and a generally recognized prophet in the larger religion that is American politics.

Wallace, however, a Southern Democrat attempting to make a name for himself outside of the Yellowhammer state, positioned himself to be a champion for white southerners and a warrior for segregation. You know, 'cause that scream "you're gonna know my name real soon so help me." Soon after Wallace gave his infamous speech calling for "segregation forever," white supremacists bombed a Montgomery church killing several young children as a way to intimidate the civil rights movement. What did Wallace do in the wake of that as governor of Alabama? He told a *New York Times* reporter: "what this country needs is a few first-class funerals, and some political funerals too." Dick move if you ask me.

One man dreamed of a nation for all people, while the other dreamed of a nation for some people, or at least that is what we know from the history books. Life is complicated, and the people we read about in the history books lived lives outside the moments we remember them for. History is meant to give us a peek into our existence and show us our past so we can chart out our future. Sometimes, those who dream of the future don't have the chance to see it, and those who desperately hang onto the past are dragged forward to tomorrow whether they like it or not.

Bobby Kennedy, the champion of the suffering and the knight of virtue who would rebuild Camelot, was shot and killed at the Ambassador Hotel in California on the night of the vital California primary for the 1968 Democratic nomination for president. Four years later, at a public event for his own 1972 presidential campaign, George Wallace was shot in Maryland by an assassin who didn't place his shots right, leaving Wallace alive but severely wounded for the remainder of his life. The difference between both shootings when you look at public reaction according to most historians is that Americans across the nation were genuinely saddened by the death of Bobby. Barry Goldwater, aka "Mr. Conservative", even shed a tear for the death of both Kennedys whom he considered close friends. For George on the other hand, some prayed, some were indifferent, and others felt it was unfair the assassin's bullets didn't get the job done the way they did with John, Bobby, and Martin Luther King. In the grand scheme of cosmic injustices, for many, this was a middle finger aimed directly at decent people as it was announced George Wallace would live another day.

With Bobby, many dream of what would have been if he had lived and continued his campaign on the road to the White House. In regards to George, others often speculate how unfair the universe is that his assassin failed and Bobby's succeeded.

The Kennedy era is long gone, and George Wallace is in the ground pushing up daisies. The issues we face today, however, haven't changed. Today, we are still questioning whether the dreams of MLK and Bobby have come to fruition. We find ourselves dealing with a war that has lasted longer than Vietnam. Communism and its twisted sister socialism are making a comeback as well, thanks to the Latina babe from New York and the self-hating billionaire from Vermont. Politics though, is still, and has always been, unfair. In my eyes, I see more George Wallaces today than I do Bobby Kennedys. Maybe I'm a pessimist, or maybe I just know better.

Given the current attitude of hatred and antipathy towards fellow men, I doubt Americans could even pray for one another if another leader were to be gunned down by an assassin. After the 2017 Alexandria shooting at the Republican practice for the annual Congressional baseball game, everyone pointed fingers at each other for causing it. A year later, Republican Senator Rand Paul (who was present at the Alexandria shooting) was assaulted in his front yard while mowing his lawn, almost resulting in death. Many liberal publications jumped the gun, and without even looking at an ounce of facts, published various op-eds saying Paul had it coming. Every day online, you can very easily find people wishing violence upon one another. The world is a rather disturbing place, and we have replaced our concept of respect with the pursuit of control and winning by any means necessary. If you ever want to ask whether humanity needs another flood of biblical proportions, go read the comments section of any video on YouTube and within a few minutes, you'll be praying for either a rapture or another series of plagues.

You might not like politics or want it to have any role in your life, but it does. For many Americans on both sides of the aisle, politics is a civil religion; it is the new pop culture. It used to be something we talked about a few times a year when we were forced to, but other than that we had actual interests. If you truly dissect it, American politics has its own religious worldview structure too. Man is incredibly dangerous left on his own; as a result, we have the State. Man's sin is simply living; hence, we must pay taxes. Our elected leaders are the most righteous among us; therefore, they lead. Then there is the struggle, there is good and evil, us and them, and anyone not with us is against us and consequently lacks any redeeming human qualities. Hillary Clinton made this apparent when she called people not voting for her "irredeemable" and "deplorable." One side can't let the other side take control for a minute, or else the whole freaking world might end next week.

I can't tell you what would have happened if Bobby Kennedy's wounds hadn't taken his life. I can't tell you things would have been sunshine and rainbows if he stayed in the race and became president. I can tell you, how evil takes roots, the exact cost of winning when principles are sacrificed, how one moment doesn't have to define a man's entire life, even though the history books say something very different.

Success in politics is all about one thing: legacy. It's all about the final destination. If you know that one thing, that will tell you everything you need to know about how the sausage is made. Nothing should surprise you if you know another person's true intentions at the end of the day: good or bad.

Bobby Kennedy's life came to an end on that night, without a doubt, changing the course of American history. George Wallace's life, as he laid on the gravel bleeding with several bullets lodged in his torso, would end in one form and continue in another. The George Wallace who made a Faustian bargain in order to succeed in politics would essentially die on that day. The George Wallace that woke up the next day recovering in the hospital however, that George Wallace, would go on to live a life not included in the history books.

Wallace would learn very clearly that success in politics is actually pretty easy, but being successful at answering the question of one's purpose of living is a different beast altogether.

CHAPTER 2

Better than Booze

C heap whiskey has a certain smell to it as it combines with your sweat, as it comes out of your pores. I'm a sloppy drunk when I touch alcohol, and I am not proud of that, especially when I catch a whiff of my own smell after a night of boozing and working (a winning combination). I have been very, very embarrassingly drunk on only a few occasions, most of which were in private. I'm not an alcoholic and I don't really touch liquor without a reason even in social settings. But man, I will admit I got pretty messed up on November 8th, 2016. The good news is, I was surrounded by a bunch of other drunks and alcoholics, so I don't feel too bad.

Word to the wise, a shot of Jim Beam and a whole can of Red Bull can help you achieve the best of both worlds. The whiskey helps you tolerate people, and the energy drink makes you efficient. A smiling man who is productive can make it out of any shitty workplace alive and well enough to tell the tale.

I had been working sixty-hour weeks for two months, and on the final days of the 2016 election, I don't remember sleeping unless I could steal a few minutes to nap in my car between assignments. I got very good at changing clothes in my car too, but one day I was so tired I walked out with a button down shirt with a tie and blazer, and my college sweatpants still on. Remarkably, I was cognizant enough to at least tuck my shirt into my sweatpants. I couldn't let the interns or volunteers know I was out of my wits, so I worked the entire afternoon with the sweatpants still on. I like to think the outfit said, "I'm a professional but I also like to be comfortable." The humor was lost on some people with squinty and judgmental faces thinking one man in a sweatpants/business combo will ruin the entire campaign's reputation.

On Election Day, in a city that folks like myself from the Beltway never ventured to, a stereotypical nowhere town in Virginia, a kid walked up to my car window, where I was sleeping in plain view with my mouth open and drool pouring onto my wrinkled suit jacket. I was about to peel my eyes open to get on the road and make my 1pm meeting with a local radio station in a town three hours away. "Mommy is that man homeless?" The kid asked his mother as he pointed to me in the driver's seat. The mother came by and put a dollar bill under my windshield wiper, assuming I was perhaps a well-dressed homeless man who must have been offended by her harshly honest son.

"Don't point at the homeless man while he sleeps" she told him. It would have been funny if the kid could have seen the two dudes in my backseat snoring. I called them my "Dream Team", my two political prodigies who were working as my personal campaign hit squad. Need a staged photo op? Need a thousand doors hit by this afternoon? Need us to go make it look like young people actually want to vote Republican? We were your go-to guys. The three of us carpooled on the way down the day prior. Our assignments were simple that day. Dwayne, our African American colleague, would go to the predominantly black portion of the town and see if anyone needed instructions on how to get to their polling place. We couldn't have sent Colin, the walking, talking Ken doll, or else he would have been shot for smiling at the wrong person in the wrong neighborhood (Dwayne's verdict, not mine, even though I was thinking it too).

Colin has what some would describe as an "assault smirk", a constant smile that suited his handsome face but let off an air of white entitlement if you knew nothing about him. I didn't even like him the first time I met him, but the kid grows on people. Colin was a humble person who could get along with everyone, but he was a Republican operative so he had the Mitt Romney look down in spades. Therefore, we had to send him to places we knew he wouldn't get stabbed for simply existing, like grocery stores near retirement communities and Moose Lodges. Instead we had Colin borrow a vehicle and drive the elderly to vote, a much safer plan.

We were contracted to work for a Republican candidate running for Congress. He was pretty popular, but Trump wasn't; therefore, we all had targets on our backs as we worked that day, as we did the entire campaign. It's funny looking back. Trump haters called me a self-hating Mexican (I'm not Mexican), Dwayne was an "Uncle Tom," and I remember someone calling Colin a "Brock Turner lookalike." This campaign, like many others across the country, was tied to Trump at the hip whether we liked it or not, and people all around the district let us know how they felt about him.

"I hope you choke on shit and die," a woman told me outside one voting location as she drove off in her beat up Pinto and flipped me the middle finger; a total class act. A look into her purse probably would have shown a Planned Parenthood punch card; buy ten abortions get the eleventh free.

"All I can say is if you don't vote for Trump, you're voting against America," one volunteer said to another at our headquarters while sipping on coffee, which would spill onto and stain his homemade Trump fan club tee shirt. This is what I was dealing with, there was no middle ground on Trump. He was Christ or Lucifer, and you better not call him Adam.

"Fuck!" Dwayne woke up yelling, "We need to get ready to head to the GOP victory party. It's a four-and-a-half-hour drive." He was right, and I needed to get to my radio interview on the other side of the district so I could seduce some on the fence voters to show up and cast a ballot. I knew Trump wouldn't win Virginia, but Trump wasn't my boss, the future Congressman from our district was. "Art, we gotta move man," he said to me.

I drove like a bat out of hell, at one point going twenty over so I could blast past a yellow light. I shouldn't have been driving; I had little to no rest the last several days, and I had taken some serious migraine medication that could tranquilize a bear. Colin was in the front seat giving me directions while Dwayne sprawled across the back seat to catch some fleeting moments of sleep. "Colin, where do I make my turn?" I asked with my eyes dead set on the road. He was quiet, the movement of the car rocked him to sleep like a baby. "Colin! Wake the fuck up, we're about to crash!" We weren't crashing but I knew that would wake him up.

If he hadn't worn a seatbelt, I'm convinced he would have jumped through the windshield. He flung his arms as I freaked him out, and his phone was flung directly into Dwayne's face. "Goddammit! Who the fuck did that!" Dwayne yelled.

"Man, my fault, my fault" Colin said, worrying about whether Dwayne's face was alright but also concerned he may have cracked his phone. I looked at the rearview mirror to see Dwayne's hilariously pissed off face, and noticed my bloodshot eyes looking back at me. This car was a powder keg of frustration and anger waiting to explode, but laughing at Dwayne's pain even made Colin chuckle, which lightened the mood for at least a minute as we drove down the country roads.

"Colin, if you weren't guaranteeing us the female vote, I'd fuck up your face for that." Dwayne laid back down but was obviously paranoid another phone would go flying at him again the moment he got comfortable. "I had old Democrats throw less expensive shit at me during this campaign dammit." Colin, despite looking like an Abercrombie and Fitch model, was a very quiet and personable human being, the type of guy everyone wanted to be friends with. It also didn't hurt that women were attracted to Colin like a sex magnet. I'm pretty sure Colin brought us more women to register to vote when we tabled on college campuses than the entire local GOP managed to pull that year.

At a fundraiser a month prior, I brought Colin to hobnob with the affluent. A much older woman came over to me as I was trying to fix my Bluetooth headset so I could make work calls and drink at the same time. She was holding two glasses of wine so I knew something was afoot. "Excuse me, are you Art Brown? The Congressman's youth coordinator?" a soft, female voice that belonged to the tall woman standing behind me asked. I said yes, and she lit up with a big smile. "Is your friend old enough to drink?" She asked me while looking straight at Colin who was talking to some state senator's daughter. The woman was probably in her sixties, but the makeup, clothes, and obvious plastic surgery made her look from a considerable distance like she was in her thirties. She had donated enough money to put up a dozen large Trump signs in every neighborhood across the county, so we had to treat her well.

"He's not twenty-one but he's old enough to have fun," I said to her with a teasing wink. The woman blushed and gave me the second glass of wine, then proceeded to go see if her cougar skills could snatch up Colin. It was a classic dingo stealing a baby scenario, and I watched from afar as Colin went from charming and polite to visibly uncomfortable as the woman stood closer and began to rub his back. A foot taller than him, she utilized her short, tight, low cut dress and had her cleavage right up against his face as she laughed at his jokes and pulled him closer. He gave off a nervous laugh and started looking around to find a way out. He turned around for a moment and looked at me and I smiled, lifted my glass to cheer him on, and walked away so I could leave him with the woman. I needed to raise more money; therefore, Colin would have to take one for the team and treat the nice rich lady well. Meanwhile, Trump needed more signs.

"Guys," Colin said on the way back from that fundraiser, "I think that woman wanted to seduce me, and she's following me on Snapchat now." I started laughing, the kid was so oblivious.

"She was, and if you gave the nice lady what she wanted we could have gotten the Congressman some nice new flyers or commercials, too. Justify our existence on this campaign." From that point on, Colin was known as our "honeypot." If we needed more women for something, Colin was our tool. As long as we didn't tell him our plan, everything worked perfectly. We were part of the youth element of the campaign, and that meant getting lazy millennials to take an interest in politics for no pay and zero benefits long enough to help us win. The secret is if there were women, especially cute women, single men showed up and worked like their lives depended on it. Promise cute women and free pizza, and you have yourself an army. It works for cults, and it works for politics.

The radio interview was brief, maybe only two minutes. I gave a five-minute pitch about the economy and other puff policy, but all they aired was "go out and vote Republican today." The radio jockeys and reporters set up a booth outside the polling place at some college deep in Trump country. From the looks of the crowds throwing stickers and flyers at passersby, you would have thought there was a Brad Paisley concert in town. A bunch of students set up cardboard boxes in a row and asked voters to "sign Trump's wall." There were a group of Libertarians standing outside for Gary Johnson, old men who thought the kids would be down with Gary and "Wild Man" Bill Weld. The Hillary Clinton volunteers were sitting on a bench drinking Starbucks. They knew this wasn't their crowd, so why bother at all?

I ran in, and within a hot minute I ran out. My radio clip was pretty worthless but still, it counted, and I was the one asked to do it. A good trooper does as he's told no matter how much time it wastes. I doubt a single voter woke up that day not knowing who to vote for; my plea wasn't going to change that at all. This wasn't American Idol, I don't think anyone was on the fence about either candidate, and most Americans don't even know who it is they are voting for down-ballot; they just vote straight party so why even bother being educated?

Dwayne was standing near a food truck on the curb a few feet away talking to a few college girls. "Yeah, so as the youth coordinator for the congressman, I've got to be his eyes and ears on the ground, guide him so he knows our perspective, you get what I'm saying?" He said as he took off his fake, Malcolm X glasses to wipe them as a sign of hard work and intellect. He didn't need those glasses to see, he bought them so he could be taken more seriously by others. I sent him a text telling him to get his ass back to the car so we could grab Colin and leave. "Excuse me ladies, I have to go make America great again."

"Did you tell them you had my job?" I asked him.

"Absolutely" he replied.

"Did it work?"

"Absolutely." We fist-bumped each other and walked back to my car. I wasn't gonna get angry over a brother trying to put the moves on someone. I dropped the Dream Team off at Colin's apartment where they jumped in his car. From there I had to pick up my girlfriend Sabrina, wrap up whatever loose ends I could at the campaign office, and drive another several hours to the location of the victory party. There were only two hours left until the polls closed, so whatever was going to happen was going to happen regardless of whatever I could do in those last remaining moments before history was made.

I was Slim Pickens from *Dr. Strangelove* during that long ride, straddling a spiritual atomic bomb getting ready to land on some unsuspecting population. Each vote in America felt like a bullet in a gun. That day, everyone was taking aim at each other, blasting away so they could force their view of the world on everyone else. No matter why people voted the way they did, the ticket would be cast either way, the barrel of the gun would be smoking, and there are no take backs. I gladly took money from the Republicans, but I always voted third party as a silent form of protest. Because I knew they'd never win, I'd never have to be responsible for any bad or disastrous decisions they made.

All over conservative talk radio, I was told people like me damned the country to a thousand-year Reich, where one half of the country would essentially become Mad Max's Thunderdome and the other half was RoboCop's Detroit. I would imagine sometimes while listening to the radio Sean Hannity and I locked in a room, looking at two switches on a wall. I know one switch activates an Earth-shattering bomb and the other doesn't. Hannity is yelling at me on one side into my ear while a whole army of *CNN* reporters are next to the other ear screaming, both causing me to go deaf. There ultimately was no third choice. I just wanted the yelling to end and their spit to stop hitting my face. To end it all I pull down both levers, everything goes away in a hot, white flash and I'm pulled out of that midday nightmare. Neither of them should ever be in any position of power, and it's sickening how they turn everything into a life or death scenario.

Liberals online, on air, and on TV weren't much nicer, but in their minds they had the election in the bag, and many of us believed it. Depending on whose side won, the losers would be forced into concentration camps. If conservatives got their way, liberal arts majors would be put into slavery and forced to build the wall. If Hillary won, everyone else would be sent to Siberian re-education camps and forced to wear pantsuits. Either way tomorrow was going suck for someone, but I was so emotionally numb I didn't care. I had done everything I could for my race, and those results were the only ones I cared about.

Virginia had gone bright Democrat blue a long time ago. The national campaign didn't matter to the commonwealth in the slightest, and it didn't matter to me.

I turned the radio on. The local station said, "Experts are predicting a Clinton victory with 98% certainty." So, I did what any sane American would do. I put my iPhone playlist on shuffle and started the remainder of my road trip with Death of a Bachelor by Panic at the Disco!. Sabrina, dressed in her nice, new, black cocktail dress, fell asleep after I picked her up from her apartment. She'd had a long day, but I was so busy talking about mine I didn't even know what exactly had tired her out. The lyrics of the song danced in my delirious mind as I tried desperately to stay awake while not letting the pressures of the day give me a panic attack. One part of the song really stood out to me, however:

The death of a bachelor...

Oh oh oh...

Seems so fitting for...

the happy ever after...

How could I ask for more?

I imagined myself in the music video, dressed in a tux in a black-and-white movie, dancing and singing in an empty bar impressing no one but myself. In a strange way, my daydream was a way of me trying to tell myself that at the end of the day, I'd still be okay, despite whatever changed tomorrow. I'm married to tomorrow no matter what. This was the long road coming to an end. An election cycle like no other in history, and my only job was just to do the best I could and nothing more. The Dream Team and I accomplished great things in a short amount of time, and for that we had already made a name for ourselves during the campaign. I knew regardless of the outcome tonight, the three of us would still be rock stars in the morning. Worst case scenario unemployed, but still rock stars.

Sabrina and I arrived a few moments after Colin and Dwayne did. We were relieved the driving was over with for the day. The campaign had rented us all hotel rooms in town knowing it was going to be a late night. We walked over to the entrance of the bar, and immediately the crowd of staff, volunteers, and supporters looked at us and began to cheer. A bunch of guys from a bunch of different campaign offices came over to shake our hands. "You're the team we kept seeing on Facebook! We saw everything you guys were doing, and we're really impressed with your Get Out To Vote effort" one person said to us. This was 2016, live-streaming on Facebook for the general user was now accessible, so we took full advantage of that and other things traditional youth initiatives ignored. The wave of the future, baby. If it looked cool, we wanted to try it out.

The bar was crowded, and the alcohol was flowing. Other staffers kept coming over to me, offering to buy me shot after shot. Contrary to popular belief, the cool and loose Art Brown everyone around me thought they knew had rarely touched alcohol up until this point, but tonight I was gonna cut loose since it wasn't my tab getting pounded. "You gotta have a beer with me, man," my short supervisor, Paul Domingo, said as he came over and hugged me from behind. "You've accomplished great things with your team and you deserve to be celebrated no matter what happens tonight." That night couldn't have gone any other way. For most of my political career I was on the losing end, so as I sat down next to Sabrina I sipped my beer and tried to shut out everything around me. I was in a crowd full of people but mentally I wanted silence, I wanted the whole thing to be over.

But not so soon.

Our candidate won by an eight-point margin, and within an hour, Donald J. Trump was the President-Elect. Hillary was down, the demon-bitch was finally slain. Now we just had to see what a President Donald Trump really led like. Paul came over, missing his suit jacket and wearing his tie around his head like a bandana. "We won, motherfuckers, we won!" he yelled as a group of some of the college-aged volunteers started cheering and dancing. It was so surreal. My only thought was that I needed more alcohol.

"Brown! Art Brown!" One slender guy wearing a seersucker suit yelled as he walked up to me, "I've been keeping up with everything your team did. We should keep up with each other and see if we can collaborate in the future," he said. I smiled, took the card he gave me and put it in my back pocket. I didn't even know his name or what he did on the race exactly, but that's what cards are for. He walked over to a tall girl in a short, black skirt at the bar and put his arm around her as they watched the news on the TV. I'm good at reading people, and I could tell they weren't together, but with the way he kept filling her up with alcohol he wanted to change that status, at least temporarily. He slid his arm down her back and tried to place his hand on her ass. She quickly turned around and walked away the moment he got a handful of her.

Ten minutes later some announcements were made, the Congressman-elect made a speech, and then the campaign manager, Bart Keller, gave out some other words no one paid attention to or remembered. The man in seersucker came back and loudly said to a crowd at the bar, "I just got a call. I'm on the Trump transition team!" More cheers, more beer to go around, this round on him of course. The girl in the black skirt who walked away earlier completely changed her demeanor and attitude. She came back, and within a minute his hand was where he wanted it the entire time. I chuckled. Looking at them, I knew their strange partnership had a clear expiration date.

"Mr. Brown, good to meet you tonight!" Another man came over. This time I recognized him. His last name was Malin and he was one of the primary staff who worked out of the local office. "Heard you on the radio today. We gotta talk after the party dies down and figure out when you're running for office." I was flattered, but I wasn't taking it very seriously. However, to this day, I still don't know if he really meant it or if he was just trying to be nice.

Outside the bar, I heard yelling. A group of teenage volunteers had drawn a picture of Hillary Clinton on some pumpkins and someone had managed to unscrew an American flag with the pole attached from the outer wall of the bar. They dropped the pumpkins on the floor and started to beat them until they were mush, flag side up obviously for Instagram. They waved their MAGA hats in the air and cheered cries of victory. An outside observer and a better storyteller would break down the group mentality, try and explain the inner workings of young men in a state of bliss on the night of what many consider a political revolution, and go on to say it was a physical manifestation of toxic masculinity or some other buzzword. I was too drunk to care and still only remember seeing that whole situation as teens being teens. Sometimes people do stuff for the sake of it, nothing else implied.

There was a beautiful, African-American reporter in a tight red dress there that night doing interviews. I knew her from the local paper, and knew she was also a liberal. She was smart though, a red dress amongst Republicans is good camouflage. Dwayne followed her around trying to get her number, but she was more interested in getting a quote from the Congressman-elect, and by the way she walked over to Malin and stroked his arm, a one-on-one exclusive with a man who was almost guaranteed a spot in Washington. Dwayne walked over and ordered more drinks for Colin, Sabrina, and me.

"I hope we get separate rooms, man, cause everyone is hot, happy, and horny tonight," Dwayne said before chugging his beer. Colin and I looked at each other and started laughing. "What's so funny?"

"Due to scarce campaign resources the three of us will be sharing two king size beds and Sabrina is gonna share a room with a female staffer," Colin told him before downing a shot of Jim Beam. The kid had turned twenty-one a week before the election so he was trying out different drinks like a man who'd never seen food before would sample a buffet.

An hour later we left the bar, and as the Dream Team and I walked like zombies to our Uber while Sabrina grabbed a ride with her roommate, I saw the man in the seersucker swapping spit with a shorter redhead in a white cocktail dress. It was kind of funny; it just proved that this guy who couldn't get a girl to look at him this morning was suddenly an eligible bachelor plotting out his own manifest destiny. Obviously, the tall girl in the black skirt didn't want it bad enough, but the short redhead was willing to take her place with some added enthusiasm.

We arrived at the Red Roof Inn across town. We each had our room keys in hand but the three of us were too hammered to properly read the numbers. Somehow, each of us thought we saw a different number than the one that was clearly engraved on our keys, so we stumbled around trying to find room sixty-three separately as we bickered about how to find it. Colin walked up two stories and ended up in the hundreds section while Dwayne walked circles in the parking lot, talking to himself about how he could potentially be called to be the Secretary of State. "Chicks love the Secretary of State," Dwayne said on repeat a dozen times while removing articles of clothing one at a time. All I could think of was taking off my sweaty blazer I had worn for days and taking a cold shower.

I saw a door cracked open next to room sixty-three. Don't ask me why, but something in the back of my mind told me to open it and walk in. I did, and directly in front of me I saw Malin and the reporter stark naked fornicating like animals. I was so shocked it was happening right in front of me, I'm pretty sure I went blind for a second and dropped my room key while they did the vertical tango in order to establish positive relations between the new representative's office and the local press. I could tell they had been drinking, thus the door being open and their failure to acknowledge me standing right there watching them. The liberal media wasn't an enemy of Republicans in that moment, that was for sure. A year later, he got fired and she wrote op-eds saying Republicans were killing people by destroying Obamacare. Back to that moment: luckily they were too drunk and distracted to know I walked in on their exclusive interview. I quickly walked backward and shut the door after picking up my key.

"Baby, come cuddle with me" I heard a girl say in the hallway. I looked over my shoulder and saw Colin trying to push a woman away from him. She was a secretary for one of the College Republican groups, and she was, by the looks of it, more hammered than all of us. Curvy, blonde, and wearing a dress which showed ample cleavage, she was a guaranteed eye-catcher. I'm still surprised Colin was able to hold himself back. "Baby, don't you wanna play with me?" She said to him. Colin convinced her to go to her room, and he then began to speed walk over to my direction. I was proud of him. He was a symbol of chivalry and Christian virtue in a world where the University of Virginia frats were labeled rape central by Rolling Stone and all drunk men were essentially considered sexual predators, even though she was the hammered one on the hunt. Colin was kind and smart. He was too young for a future #MeToo scandal.

"I think that girl was trying to sleep with me," Colin said, rubbing his bloodshot, alcohol glazed eyes. I laughed hysterically. It shocked me a guy so handsome and smart could be so oblivious to women.

"Maybe you should have taken her up on it man, you and Dwayne are sharing a bed," I said.

"You're an asshole, Art," Colin said jokingly.

"I'm the asshole who's gonna get us all jobs in the morning," I replied.

Dwayne and Colin grabbed a spot on the end of each bed and turned on the TV so they could see the remaining states go for Trump. I turned the shower on cold and listened to them laugh as my least favorite person on TV, Van Jones from CNN, began to cry about some people waking up to a "nightmare." I wish I could have bottled up his salty, liberal tears and drank them in front of a crowd of weeping Democrats. This was our victory, and I wasn't going to apologize for basking in it. If Hillary and the woman we ran against in the district had won, I doubt they would have acted differently. This is politics: there is only winning and losing, and losers don't legislate. It sucks to suck, simple as that.

It was 4 am. We had officially been awake for 48 hours at that point and Trump had broken the blue wall in the north-east and secured the White House. Malin and the reporter on the other side of the wall stopped knocking boots hours ago and must have fallen asleep. Dwayne slept on the floor while Colin slept with his suit still on underneath the covers. I opted to fill the tub full of cold water. I was too drunk to step out and too tired to care. I felt a dip in the cold tub would do me good, and I'm too tall to have drowned so I didn't worry about that either. I looked over to the toilet seat lid where I set my phone and saw it going off with a barrage of text messages. The texts could wait. The life of this bachelor ended tomorrow. I'd be wed to a brave new world. I imagined myself as a legislative director or a chief of staff. Rubbing shoulders with Paul Ryan in the Speaker's office or delivering a speech to the press. I picked up a towel on the floor and hit the light switch on the wall to turn the lights off like Indiana Jones with his whip so I could sleep.

The cold water turned lukewarm, but in a few minutes it suddenly became ice cold again. I thought maybe it was the alcohol coursing through my body giving me strange readings of my temperature. I kept my eyes closed the entire time, however, until I heard a soft, quiet laughing right next to me. I opened my drunk eyes and saw the room began to spin slowly like a circus ride. Shit was about to get weird.

Sitting on the toilet was a man with red skin and a white suit, with short horns sticking out of his forehead, looking at me like some circus freak. I was shocked for a second but I realized even in that moment that this was all a product of consuming one, two, seven too many drinks, copious amounts of migraine medication, stress, and sheer exhaustion.

All that, and I realized I recognized the red bastard, so it must have been fake. I could recognize the prince of darkness anywhere.

"Richard Nixon?" I asked, while rubbing my eyes trying to wake myself up. He laughed some more.

"You can call me that, or Satan, or Satan Nixon, or President Devil, just don't call me Tricky Dick," he said. "I'm your hallucination so call me whatever you want, Art." We just kinda stared at each other for a minute, I was hoping I would wake up from whatever twisted headspace I was in. "I'm just here to tell you I'm so excited to work together. You're finally going places little buddy, and I hope you've learned a thing or two about how nice it is to be liked for once and win something this big."

"Yeah I mean it's pretty cool" I said, "but why do you look like Satan, Nixon...Satan? This is victory night so why can't you look like Katy Perry or Mia Khalifa instead?" He kept laughing at me as if I was walking into a joke, ready to become the punchline of this psychotic breakdown.

"Because deep down inside you know you're gonna end up like all those little bastards back at the bar, all future senators and present-day ass kissers who would drown their grandma to be the ambassador to East Timor." Satan Nixon got down on a knee and looked me directly in the eyes. "Call yourself a good man, but you're gonna need to listen to me to get around this new town called Winning, buddy boy," he reached behind my head and pulled out a cigarette, which he lit with a snap of his fingers.

"I've been getting around just fine man..." I tried speaking, but Satan Nixon interrupted me.

"You think they give out Nobel Peace Prizes for free, bitch? They make those medals by hand, sucker, and you knew one day you'd win and you wouldn't know how to properly handle it, which is why I'm here. I've always been here. A product of man's animal brain so they can justify asshole decisions to each other. I was there when God crapped out the third caveman so I could convince one of them there was a conspiracy formed by the others." He threw his cigarette in the bathtub and the water got warmer. "You think that ugly inbred in the room next door scored that honey he brought to bed with him because he's genuinely interesting?"

"It certainly wasn't his personality," I said.

"You better believe it. That guy would have made a great employee in the Nixon White House," he said. "But enough talk. I'll be here waiting for you, just like everyone else. Everyone has a little devil on their shoulder who they ask for a list of ways to screw over everyone around them." I was getting nervous; this beer battered hallucination was going on too long for my liking.

"This is different, everything is going to be different. I trust the people around me..." I said only to be interrupted again as the water in the tub began to boil and the room spun faster.

"And they trust you to be weak. They're gonna suck the life out of you and skin you alive unless you listen to what's what." He started laughing and I immediately felt like puking. I felt like I was flying through space in this itchy motel bathtub with that red freak beginning to fade away while laughing louder and louder. He continued laughing while extending his arms out giving that classic Nixon victory sign in each hand, yelling "Welcome to politics, bitches!" as the whole room went pitch dark.

I feel like I should have learned some lesson if this experience was my subconscious mind really speaking to me. Instead, I closed my eyes and passed out.

Remso W. Martinez

CHAPTER 3

Killing Baby Hitler

Satan Nixon was on my mind the next day as I woke up and struggled to tell the difference between hallucination and reality. The tub water was lukewarm, and I was as pruned as a raisin. It was time for us to leave town and return home to patiently wait for whatever misadventures were ahead for us.

Sabrina and I tuned into the local talk radio station to listen to the world's reaction to this new example of American democracy in action. The guy from *the Apprentice* defeated the Queen of the Establishment class. "What strange times we live in," I said to her. I looked over to see her reaction, but she was asleep once again. Apparently, the drunk blonde who was trying to hit on Colin in the hallway was her roommate last night, so she got absolutely no sleep. She'd stayed up worrying the drunk chick would need a ride to a hospital.

"Donald Trump is the reincarnation of George Wallace!" A man on the radio was yelling. "This man dog whistles pure racism and is only gonna take care of some of the country, not all of the country, and you know what I'm talking about when I say some people." That kind of shocked me, the part where he decided to call Trump the reincarnation of George Wallace instead of Hitler, or Mussolini, the two despot fascists most often compared to Trump as they tried to paint him as the worst humanity had to offer.

Call a man Hitler and it doesn't mean anything. People are called Hitler for cutting in line at Starbucks. Call a man Mussolini and some people might not even know who he is. Now, you call a man George Wallace, and that means something deep, and purely evil. American history doesn't have too many homemade villains, but George Wallace is a person virtually all Americans unite in hating. Calling Trump a racist is common for his haters, but call him a racist segregationist like George Wallace and that is an upgraded insult to a man which implies no socially redeemable qualities.

I wondered as we drove back while Sabrina slept, what did the Satan Nixon standing on George Wallace's shoulder say to make him the way he was?

Just like every other human being, George Wallace was at one point in time, if you could believe it, a baby. It is weird to think that all villains start life as innocent infants who can't comprehend the concept of hate at all. During the GOP primaries, Governor Jeb Bush said if he could go back   in time, he would kill baby Hitler. Yes, Hitler was a monster, he was literally Hitler, but a baby Hitler? For one, I've seen far too many time travel films to know that plan never works out well for anyone. One day you find a way to go instantly back in time and kill baby Hitler, then you go back to the present and some other Nazi took his place as the evilest man in history. Go back to try and fix it by going further back in time and kill Hitler's father, then you return to the present a second time and an alien species of intelligent squids with submachine guns are storming Washington D.C. Time travel is weird; don't ever mess with that stuff.

George Corley Wallace grew up in a quiet town called Clio, Alabama to working-class parents. His family was poor, but according to his mother, "We'll never have to worry about putting food on the table." His grandfather was the town doctor, and when George was a child, he would attend patient visits with his grandfather around town. Black, white, Grandpa Wallace didn't discriminate. To him, they were all part of the working poor; poverty and hardship was color blind. It was business as usual to pay him in fresh eggs or a pig. However his patients could pay was good enough for him.

This lesson stuck hard to young George very early on in his childhood. The developing southern economy was a hard world for the working class. He saw how exploitative labor practices combined with big northern companies coming to Alabama for cheap labor helped some climb the economic ladder, but also crushed the homegrown competition. Alabama-born businesses just couldn't keep up with market forces. For the young progressive, it became very clear the struggle between the working class and the wealthy would become an issue very close to home for him.

George wasn't poor, but he wasn't what many would consider the stereotype of the Alabama political class. His father, who worked at the polling stations on Election Day, would bring George with him to help count the ballots. This is where George first felt excited about the political process. Around town, politics was part of the culture, and often George's father would wander down to the courthouse after a hard day of work and talk politics with the other men. At around age six, some locals said George learned to introduce himself to every newcomer to town, and say "I'm George Wallace, and if you ever need any help let me know." One could only imagine a miniature Satan Nixon standing on young George's shoulder, laughing with pure joy knowing the boy would have a talent for politics as he got older.

Years later, George was accepted to the University of Alabama, where he excelled academically, and showed interest in boxing. The other boys in his class knew very little of the small town, working-class environment George had grown up in. Many of them were aspiring doctors, lawyers, businessmen, and politicians, yet they had grown up their entire lives being groomed for that mindset. George, however, always felt he had more to prove, and his way up the social ladder was going to be more difficult than the others.

Perhaps that was why he was drawn to boxing, a sport where punches flew and every man was equal in the ring. Wallace, a fiery fighter whose crooked upper lip always looked like he was aching for a fight, excelled in the ring. In many ways, boxing- because of its more personal, physically and mentally demanding nature- is the perfect metaphor for politics and Wallace's direct approach to things. I win, you lose, only one person was going to walk out of the ring victorious, and he knew in his mind it would be him. If you dare take a shot at the king, you better not miss.

As Governor of Alabama, Wallace put up an enlarged, framed photo of one of his fights against the wall near his desk. Most people will put up family photos, diplomas, inspirational cat posters with a message like "hang in there!" But not George. The photo showed Wallace, with his infamous right hook, knocking out an opponent whose mouth burst open with a glob of blood flying through the air. That photo said all you need to know about him: he's gonna hit you and make it count. You could be friends outside the ring, but inside you know that there can only be one winner.

After graduating with his law degree from Alabama, George met the much younger but incredibly charming Lurleen Burns. It was a strange relationship, her very quiet and George being much more of an opinionated extrovert. George was a fighter with a chip on his shoulder and grand aspirations. She was a quiet tomboy who was still in her teens when she met the adult Wallace. It was a Beauty and the Beast scenario, except the Beast in the tale didn't have a choice in being a monster; George willingly chose to go into politics.

"Politics is something daddy talks about with the other men," Lurleen once said when asked about her political views. In a way, they filled out each other's deficiencies, which was easy since they were smitten with each other. George, a cocky brawler who knew every shopkeeper and chicken thief in the county by name, and Lurleen, the quiet southern belle. He needed someone to show compassion; she needed someone to fight for her. Perhaps Beauty and the Beast isn't a good example for this love story, because that story had a happy ending.

In 1946, George's dream came true, and he won his first election for the Alabama House of Representatives. The brawler was in the ring, and conservative Republicans, hardline segregationists, and big business Democrats were his opponents. For George, despite his craving for power, he always remembered that to many of the affluent he would always just be a redneck country boy. George never tried to outrun his past. Instead, he embraced it and made it a cornerstone of his political and public identity. In George's stump speeches, he made an effort to bring out blacks to listen. Young George didn't separate between the poor whites and poor blacks. For him, the struggles of the working poor were colorblind, and that was all he needed to know.

On more than one occasion he was described as too progressive for his own good. He advocated for lofty work and welfare programs similar to what FDR had done in George's youth. For many of his Democrat colleagues, Wallace just seemed different. They even called him a socialist because of the lengths he was willing to go to in order to pillage the wealthy to provide for those in poverty. Under Democrat Governor Jim Folsom, who was a personal and professional mentor to Wallace,

George asked for an appointment to the board of trustees for the Tuskegee Institute, not something white people requested—ever.

Wallace's progressive streak rubbed many hardline, segregationist Dixiecrats the wrong way, but they knew he was onto something, whether they wanted to admit it or not. You see, in boxing, all viewers ever really focus on is where the punches land and where the blocking occurs. Any boxer will tell you an underestimated aspect of a fight is footwork, positioning yourself so you're solid when you need to stand but also quick enough to adjust to any attack. Wallace was always thinking of where he'd need to be quick on his feet so he could lunge forward and bring home a win for the little people. Maybe he was doing what he knew in his heart to be good, or maybe he was positioning himself for a long and lofty political legacy. Either way, his fists flew and his feet were swift; Wallace was a young force to be reckoned with. Even as an elected official, Wallace wasn't lofty enough to ignore a good bar fight if it meant he could make someone bleed when they tried to mess with him.

Wallace knew that one-day black voters would become an overwhelmingly important voting bloc in Alabama, and he wanted to be the tip of the spear and have a political career that would survive a post-segregation south. This isn't the Wallace anyone ever talks about, but if they did it would make his descent into infamy far more dramatic. In 1953, Wallace was appointed as a circuit judge, where his animosity towards the wealthy and entitled reached new heights, making him a sort of Robin Hood figure amongst Alabama's poor.

"When you address Mr. Chestnut in my courtroom you will call him Mr. Chestnut, or the Plaintiff, and refusal to do so will put you in contempt of court. Do I make myself clear?" Judge Wallace once said to a wealthy industrialist's attorney in a case against a poor farmer represented by black attorney J.L Chestnut. Chestnut and his client were referred to by the Defense as "them" and "those people," angering

Wallace. Chestnut, one of the most influential civil rights lawyers in the south, thought much of this young progressive judge, and was often the victor in his rulings.

"He was the only judge to call me Mr. Chestnut in court," Chestnut said in an interview in 1998. "If I went to court asking for $50 from the defense, Wallace would have me walk out with $75 instead." For Judge Wallace, justice was colorblind. The facts of the matter ultimately decided the rulings in his court.

The next month between Thanksgiving and Christmas, life was good. The Dream Team disbanded until February when we would get together to start coming up with a plan for the upcoming primary election in June. There were going to be primary campaigns for everything from dog catcher to governor, which meant a windfall of money would come our way. For now, we partied with the winners all over Arlington, Alexandria, Washington D.C. and Annapolis as if it were going out of style. I didn't pay for my own drink for the rest of the year. I met with a few potential clients during that time and celebrated riding the wave of enthusiasm as Trump and our other Republican friends were picking out secretaries for their front desks. Meanwhile, their wives picked out the office drapes and their mistresses picked bars to hop around. It pays to be a winner because losers don't legislate.

"I've had more women walking around town with me the last month than ever before," Dwayne texted me as I was walking around Annapolis Harbor with Sabrina and some friends on a pleasant afternoon. I texted back and told him that it would only go on until Trump picked a real Secretary of State and he would have to pick another empty cabinet position to pretend to hold. I was never much of a partisan before. In fact, I saw politics as a paycheck and nothing more at that point. There were too many broken promises and false expectations from smooth-talking politicians in the past which left me icier than an arctic glacier. Something in the air felt different though. There was a pep in my step, and my head was held a little bit higher. Sabrina bought me a Make America Great Again hat to fit in with the redder Republican crowd. It was white with black lettering so it went as good with a suit as it did with jeans. I had nothing to hold me back; I was in the winners' club and everyone knew it. Once, when we were down in downtown Annapolis, there were some anti-Trump folks passing out fliers about Russian collusion.

"Excuse me sir..." One of them said as they walked over to give me some leaflet about an upcoming protest. I put my hand up to stop him in.

"Go screw off," I said as I just kept walking forward. It pays to be a winner. We walked by a bar window and I caught a clear image of my reflection, but something was off. I turned my head and saw Satan Nixon walking behind me, smiling that Devil may care smile. Either I had to change my attitude, or I had to stop drinking, and the latter wasn't going to happen, that was for sure.

The 2016 election was important for me and my consulting firm, Fuego Advocacy. I was the CEO, Employee of the Month, secretary, company driver, etc. I think you get the point. Prior to the congressional race I had taken the idealistic route, working for cheap Libertarian Party candidates running for mayor and firebrand conservatives trying to knock out entrenched incumbents in GOP primaries across the board. Did I get paid? Not always. Did we win? Never, but it felt good to try. By the time Colin and Dwayne came on when I needed organizers for the congressional race in Virginia, victory meant life or death. Finances were strained and my reputation was already trash.

The 2016 election changed all that, and finally, I had an opportunity to make it into a league of professionals. However, the Congressman- a former owner of a PR firm who recently received a doctorate in divinity- and I had the opportunity to travel together on the campaign trail pretty often, so we hit it off. The Congressman's campaign manager, Bart Keller, and I didn't work together very often. Most of the time, we were in the same room but working on different projects. Our interactions didn't go farther than a smile with a greeting or a handshake. When Bart became the chief of staff and called me in January to ask if I wanted to come in for "a talk" about my future, I thought I knew what that meant.

All my hard work, all the positive attention my Dream Team and I earned from the campaign and the state Republican Party, was finally going to benefit me long term. After I got off the phone with Bart to schedule an appointment, I took Sabrina out to an expensive dinner to celebrate at this Mexican restaurant we both loved. The time to party had come and gone. The time to get ready to work was upon me.

"Does the Congressman know that you have an appointment with Bart?" Sabrina asked me.

"I'm pretty sure he knows if his chief of staff is gonna interview someone for a job," I replied. "The Congressman loves me, I was his guy in the local press and organized some of his largest events. Besides, if I told him I was coming in to interview for a job in his office, he'd probably think I was trying to jump the order of the office. This is good. I just need to show up, smile, and remind Bart of how good we have it."

"But do you know Bart?" she asked.

"No, but Bart knows me, and that is all that matters. He reached out to me for this interview before I even thought about applying for a gig in Washington," I said. "He saw me work on the campaign trail and saw how people flocked to the boys and me on election night. Let's just be happy, things are gonna be great baby." Little did I know things would turn to shit. Two margaritas in and I was singing to the music playing throughout the restaurant. Sabrina got up to go to the restroom, and as she walked away, I saw him sitting across the room from me. Satan

Nixon, sipping on a beer, looking at me with that bastard smile once again. He raised the bottle towards me and the noise in the restaurant went silent, as if he had muted the entire place.

"Big leagues, pal," he said as his voice echoed throughout the crowded, silent restaurant. I tossed Sabrina the keys to my car as I slapped some cash on the table to settle the check.

"I need you to drive, I'm having a hard time hearing and I'm seeing Satan all around me."

The day came and I took an Uber from my apartment in Fairfax to the Longworth office building in D.C. The city is alive in a way others aren't, because there are those that walk the streets of the swamp and look like they deserve to be there, and then there are folks like me, who look uncomfortable in this alien territory. I passed through security and walked directly to the office. Men in pressed suits and brown shoes, along with women in sophisticated work attire and black nylons crisscrossed through the halls, everyone looked like they had a purpose for being there. I got to the Congressman's office, and the first face I saw sitting behind the front desk was the blonde from the hotel who tried to drag Colin back to her room. It wasn't even her face which I recognized first, but truth be told was the low-cut shirt she wore that made all the memories of that night pop back into my mind.

"Hello, sir," she said smiling from ear to ear, "can I get your name to check your appointment?" I quickly lifted my eyes from her chest to her face so she couldn't tell I wasn't always looking at her big, beautiful smile.

"Art Brown, I'm here to see Bart Keller please," I said.

"Art!" A bold, deep voice said behind me. It was the Congressman, who was waving me to come into his office. I walked in and shook his hand. He appeared genuinely happy to see me and not in that typical, political "it's nice to see you" type of tone either.

"So do I call you Doctor Congressman now that you're a PhD and a representative?" I asked him.

"No, no," he said while laughing in between words, "I found out this morning that Bart and you are getting lunch so I wanted to stick around before my next meeting to just see how you're doing before I have to run." We spoke for a minute about Sabrina, and his wife and kids before the blonde secretary came in to alert him his next committee was meeting in a few minutes. "Gotta run, Art, feel free to stop by whenever you're in town." He gave me one of those around-the-shoulder hugs and walked off. Great guy, I thought, but didn't put too much thought into it since all I was wondering was why he said Bart and I were getting lunch. It was already 3pm.

"Art," Bart said as he walked into the office, already ten minutes late for the meeting he scheduled. "Let's go talk in the Congressman's office where we'll have more privacy." I sat down in one of the chairs in front of the desk, while Bart sat in the Congressman's high-backed rolling chair. "I'm glad you could make it into town, man."

"Thank you for reaching out, I'm glad you were able to make time to speak to me." He pulled out his phone and took a minute to respond to some texts. There was an awkward minute where it was as if he forgot I was in the room.

"Oh, sorry about that, man," he said. "So where were we... what do you want to do right now? What are your plans for the future?"

"Well, sir, I'd like to transition out of consulting and perhaps could come work here in the office to add value to the legislative team. I forwarded you the resume you requested, and, as you'll see, I have the experience from working with think tanks and non-profits, along with several other campaigns..." I was about to finish my sentence before Bart started waving his hands in front of him, gesturing for me to stop.

"Art, we like you, man. I think you'd even be a great Legislative Director in the Congressman's office." Time stood still as he froze midsentence, I felt like I had for a moment stopped time and space to truly digest the fact that he just stated I would make a great Legislative Director, my dream job. Satan Nixon popped out from behind my chair with a small American flag in each hand and the sound of applause filling the room.

"Big leagues, baby!" Satan Nixon yelled in celebration before I snapped out of my egotistical daydream and started paying attention to Bart once again.

"However, you weren't part of the transition team for this office and I've already filled up all our full-time slots." Bart finished his sentence and paused. His face went from that of someone about to give someone else some really good news to that of one of fake sympathy bullshit. Like grandpa is dead, but at least you still get to live a lot longer, or some crap like that. "There are also a lot of great guys and gals in this office working nine to five on an intern status absolutely free, and it would be morally wrong for me to hire you, an outsider, instead of hiring one of those folks."

Satan Nixon popped out behind Bart's chair, with pitch black eyes and steam coming out of his ears. "Take a pen and stab this no-good shyster in the throat, Art! Do it now and make him pay for his disrespect!" I almost considered doing just that, but the non-murderer side of me also said I was about to get screwed and the best thing to do would be to end things there and walk out. Outsider? I worked all day and night for this campaign, I went from random consultant running phone banks to an instrumental part of the campaign. The Dream Team and I succeeded where others failed, and it was my leadership which helped get the results needed to win.

"So what I'm trying to say, Art, is that I can bring you on to answer the phone at the front desk and we can give you a monthly metro pass so you aren't too out of pocket at the end of the month and we'll take things from there," he finished saying with a smile. I smiled back at him, thinking of the ways I could take a stapler and beat his bald head until his skull caved in. I had to really choose my next words carefully.

"You're not hiring at all?" I asked.

"Yes sir, not at all," he replied. There was that awkward silence again, but this time there was obvious tension in the air coming from my end of the room. One wrong "go fuck yourself" could kick me out of this cushy Republican circle had I crawled on my hands and knees to get into. Agreeing to work as an unpaid intern with a bunch of inexperienced college kids would make me his puppet and a subordinate who'd have to fetch his lunch and lick his black dress shoes clean with my tongue. I didn't work as hard as I had to start from the bottom for the same team I already started on the bottom for not even six months ago.

"I'll think about your generous offer, Bart," I said, which was an outright lie. Only a moron would take a bum deal like that. "But I think I'll be getting my team at Fuego together and we'll instead be working with clients for this upcoming primary season." Bart pretended to look disappointed, but I knew it was all an act.

"Well I can't say if you walk out I'll be able to offer this deal again," he said as we both stood up. That was the final insult, I buttoned my suit and walked out.

"Don't let it hurt your head too much, Bart," I said as I was leaving. It had taken me an hour and a half thanks to traffic to get from Fairfax to Washington D.C. Plus, I had waited twenty minutes while Bart wasn't even prepared to start our meeting. All for what? Eight minutes? My entire meeting with Bart, a meeting he arranged, lasted eight minutes, and he didn't even bother offering me as much as a bottle of water.

"Perhaps he's intimidated by you," Sabrina told me as I laid my head on her lap, sprawled across my couch later that day.

"Intimidated by me? He's the chief of staff for the Congressman, and I barely make rent," I replied.

"Everyone saw your drive on that election, how you took precincts and volunteers that weren't doing anything and made them into the most effective parts of the campaign. Everyone loved the work you did, and everyone knows you and the boys gave the team a morale boost Bart certainly wasn't giving." She was right, but I didn't want to admit that a man old enough to be my father was threatened by a guy in his mid-twenties. There had to be another reason why that whole incident went down so badly for me. Like usual however, Sabrina's assessment of the whole situation was right.

"Guys," a text to our official Dream Team *DANGER* Group Chat from Dwayne said, "Bart Keller just called me and offered me a job to start as the Congressman's scheduler at the beginning of next month."

"Great job!" Colin replied with twenty smiley face emojis.

Sabrina was right. Bart wanted me out of the picture.

CHAPTER 4

In the Dark Corner of Waffle House

Anakin Skywalker and Darth Vader are the exact same person, but Star Wars fans often speak of that character as if he were actually two separate people. On one hand, you have the brave Jedi Knight and expert pilot Anakin Skywalker, as seen in Episodes I-III, and on the other, you have the epitome of evil, the black-garbed cyborg Darth Vader from Episodes IV-VI (and Rogue One: a Star Wars Story if you want to get technical). In similar fashion, George Wallace would go on to separate one part of himself from the other and force history to choose how he would be remembered.

Anakin Skywalker's dream was to be accepted as a Jedi Master, and Wallace's was to one day be Governor of Alabama. In some ways, he felt it was his birthright, since several Alabama governors had been born in his home county. It almost seemed like it was destiny. In 1958, Wallace announced he was finally going to throw his hat into the ring, and from there he competed in a harsh primary for the Democratic nomination for governor that would change Wallace into a full-on Sith Lord. To end the constant Star Wars comparisons, so that less sophisticated and cultured readers don't have to keep going on Google to look them up, I'll wrap this up by saying that if having his legs cut off and left to burn alive on the volcano planet was what turned Anakin fully into Darth Vader, than it was this election that took George Wallace and turned him into Governor Asshole-Supreme.

Wallace's main opponent in the primary was Alabama Attorney General John Patterson. This was not the type of guy you ever want to compete against. John Patterson joined the US Army in 1939, fought across Europe and North Africa in WWII, and a decade later would fight again in the Korean War. When John returned home from the service to Phenix City, Alabama, his town was known as one of the most corrupt cities in America. Crime was rampant, and the mob ran loose. John's father, Albert "Pat" Patterson, ran for Attorney General as a Democrat on a platform of wiping out organized crime and restoring law and order. Instead, shortly after receiving the nomination, Pat was murdered, and in order to avenge his father's killing, John agreed to run in his place becoming one of the harshest law enforcers in the United States.

Patterson didn't show sympathy to anyone who broke the law, but he took things as far as he could regarding black criminals. As Attorney General, Patterson once sentenced a black man to death for stealing $1.80 from a white woman's purse. He took this his cunning and fierce attitude and applied it to his campaign for governor, full foot on the gas pedal and no brakes ahead. He knew he was going to win; there was no argument or internal dispute because he was willing and capable of doing anything to ensure that outcome.

Patterson painted Wallace as a soft on crime judge who was nice to blacks and didn't have the spine to make harsh choices. Wallace tried to take the high road and emphasized his time as both a state representative and as a circuit judge to show he could work with lawmakers to get things done as well as make bold decisions. Wallace and Patterson were as opposite as they could get. Wallace was endorsed by the NAACP, while Patterson boasted from county to county that he was the chosen candidate of the KKK. Wallace held small rallies where he talked about roads, schools, and jobs, while Patterson promised to eradicate whatever crime he hadn't already smashed as Attorney General and to stand firm as a pro-segregation governor while the rest of the nation fought to end Jim Crow. The lines were cut and dry. Even Patterson's granddaughter would say almost forty years later that he ran "the most racist platform you'd ever seen." Coming from a family member, that says something.

Patterson defeated Wallace, it wasn't even close. The boxing champ, political rabble-rouser, and progressive Robin Hood that was George Wallace became a laughingstock. Lurleen, while disappointed by her husband's defeat, was at least a little happy knowing he would be home more often and could tend to their young children who rarely saw their father. George fell into a depression and dropped out of public life for about a year. Fatherhood wasn't something he was accustomed to either, and the more time he spent with his family, the less time he could spend bringing about the changes he felt only he could bring. It stings to be a loser because losers don't legislate. To have been a fly on the wall on election night when Wallace had to call Patterson to congratulate him would have certainly been interesting.

"John, congratulations on your well-earned victory."

"Thanks George...oh, George, before I go I want to tell you something real quick."

"Yes, John?"

"Go fuck yourself, George."

Wallace threw on his regular grey suit and walked to his office at the courthouse after taking an extended vacation to be at home with his family. Once there, he had his secretary phone over to his good friend and Barbour County District Attorney, Seymour Trammell, and ask him to stop by the courthouse when he had a chance. Wallace pulled out some cigars for Trammell and himself. There wasn't going to be any talk of work, nor was Wallace really intending to get any work done that day once Seymour arrived. They talked about many things. Everything came back to Wallace's defeat and his political future in the aftermath if there was any left after such an embarrassing loss.

"I tried to talk about the real issues," George said while puffing on his cigar, "I wanted to talk about new roads and funding for schools, but all anyone wanted to talk about was the race stuff." He sat up in his chair and rubbed the remaining inch of his cigar past the label into his ashtray. "You know why I lost, Seymour?"

"Why, Judge?" Trammell asked.

"Because I was out-niggered by John Patterson, and I'll tell you right here right now, I'll never be out-niggered again." Exit Anakin Skywalker, enter Darth Vader.

I was playing some Star Wars game on my iPhone as we waited for our client to arrive at our meeting at Waffle House. It was the end of January, so Dwayne had packed up to move to D.C., leaving Colin and I to work with the few clients that had approached us. I always to picked a location where I knew not many people would show up, giving us a degree of privacy, while at the same time leaving me the opportunity to at least get a meal out of the meeting if nothing else came of it. Colin couldn't do much either way. He was going back to school but stuck around with me because he needed the money.

I pick Waffle House for several reasons when meeting potential clients. First, because I love Waffle House, and I'm not afraid to admit it's my favorite restaurant. Secondly, because you can tell a lot about a client by how they interact with the place. Waffle House is different in many ways. It's almost as if the entire establishment is alive in a way. First, I observe how they walk in, because as soon as you walk into a Waffle House you could very easily be standing next to a table of people eating, and if you stand there looking uncomfortable among the hungry, working class people I can tell you're gonna be a nervous and neurotic person to deal with.

Now onto the narrow, tight booths; does he or she look uncomfortable? Have they gotten comfy and look relaxed? Trick question because no one is comfortable in Waffle House booths. The key is to look comfortable because if you can look like you're not fidgeting for leg room, then I know you can remain calm in tense or uncomfortable situations. Failure to do so alerts me to you being someone who can't keep their cool. Keeping Cool is key in every business in the world because no one wants a wreck. Lastly, what do they order? If they order nothing, even if they aren't hungry, that person is a sociopath and you should escape the premises using Jason Bourne-like parkour immediately. If they order hash browns, are they smothered, covered, and chunked? If not, that means they don't like a little bit of danger in their lives, thus they'll be less likely to take chances in life.

It was weird not having Dwayne there, but we were proud that at least one of us was making it to D.C. Most of my friends were working stiffs now, some working as staffers in Congress, others working for a cluster of non-profit groups and think tanks, waiting on invitations for those exclusive D.C. dinners and events that let you know you finally made it. I had told Sabrina that whatever campaign came up would be my last one. I'd take the money and use it as a cushion as I looked at new career fields away from the political world that I obviously needed to get away from. In my heart, I really did want to put out Fuego's light for good. I really did, but sometimes circumstances make choices for us.

The client arrived on time, and we were the only ones sitting in the dimly lit Waffle House on the side of the highway. He walked over to us and we stood to introduce ourselves. I had Colin sit next to me so I could get a good look at the prospective client. He wore a three-piece blue suit, not an easy suit to wear while attempting to get even remotely comfortable in the tight Waffle House booth. He crossed his right leg over his left, leaned back as he spread his arms out to stretch, and looked right at home. I liked this guy's style, but the horror was about to expose itself.

"Mr. Pecker..." I said before he interrupted me.

"Please, call me Gordon," he interjected.

"Well, Gordon, I want to thank you for reaching out to Fuego to see how we could help you in your campaign for city treasurer. We're looking forward to seeing how we can help you win this upcoming primary, but first do you want to go ahead and order something so we aren't discussing business around dinner with an empty stomach?" I asked.

"Nah, I'm good, man," he said.

My blood ran cold, and I was faced with a grim decision; run out of here like an exposed baby-daddy on *The Maury Show*, or hear him out. "My wife is expecting me home for dinner after this." He saved himself with that statement, but I was still on edge. If it was a lie, at least it was a reasonable one.

"So, let's get you home earlier than expected and just lay it out on the table," I said.

"So, I'm running against two other people for the Republican primary, but I'm pretty sure one of them will drop out once I formally announce tomorrow. My main opponent, Courtney Cole, is the current city registrar, and she's deeply connected to the city's elite. Big problem for her is that she's not a real Republican. She rarely votes Republican and has never shown up to work for Republican candidates. She sits out every election but is always seen smiling and taking photos at big donor parties." Pecker was handing Colin some of her flyers so we could get a look at her.

"So where do we come in?" Colin asked.

"I need folks to go around registering voters to vote in the Republican primary. Turnout is low, and during that time you'll be doing it while talking about me so I'll be in the front of their minds during this entire campaign. Secondly, I need someone to stir up positive attention for me even if that means negative attention for her." There was a pause as I thought how to reply to this.

"I need you to clarify what you mean when you say to stir up attention. We're not a hit squad," I stated. He pulled out four hundred dollar bills and placed them on the table.

"Fellas, we're dealing with a liberal running in the Republican primary, and I will be the first person to tell you she isn't a friendly competitor. I just need to know I'm hiring a team of commandos and not a couple of guys that aren't willing to win." I looked at Colin, who was looking at the cash on the table. The kid needed four new tires for his car. He needed the cash badly, as did I since clients weren't lining up at my doorstep. I grabbed the cash in front of me, and under the table passed $200 to Colin's hand.

"How much and for how long?" I asked. The client smiled, and we got down to business. I should have known that this was a race I should have stayed out of entirely, but I was blinded by the cash and the need to feel relevant. It is a difficult thing adjusting from being someone in charge and of some relative importance to not being needed. The meeting ended, and I gave Colin a ride back to his dorm. It was a quiet, awkward ride since we were both thinking the same thing but didn't want to admit this guy Gordon was a shifty dude.

"I don't feel comfortable with Pecker," Colin said.

"I'm not gonna force you to lie or do anything you're uncomfortable with, but this is a smaller race than what you're used to and small-town politics is a different animal. It is less about having the right ideas and it's more about being the person people like," I said. Later in the evening I called Sabrina and told her about Pecker. She was just as concerned as Colin was. I was at a point where I didn't care what I'd have to do if it meant I was getting paid, and my candidate won. I had bills stacking up and if this rich Republican guy was gonna help me cover them and I had to play in the mud so he didn't have to get his hands dirty, so be it. I knew firsthand politics was a dirty game, and for once I had been sanctioned to draw blood when necessary.

"Don't do anything you're going to regret," Sabrina texted me. All I told myself that night as I took a shot before falling asleep on the couch was that losers don't legislate. The next day I was out in a neighborhood registering voters and planting Pecker's name in their head. I wasn't going to bring up Courtney Colin, a competitor I didn't know much about unless a potential voter brought her up first.

"I hear she wants to give taxpayer money to illegals!" One old man tried saying to me. Do I tell this voter he's wrong? Do I look ignorant and say I don't know? Sometimes in politics, you have to double down on stupid to keep people happy.

"Wow, that's insane," I said, just to please him, yet find a tactical way to not specifically condone that statement.

"And she's gonna bankrupt the city spending our money on welfare crack whores and people who don't work." I shook my head in agreement even though on the inside I was dying to escape this conversation. After getting his signature, I walked across the street to a bus stop bench and pulled out a flask. I was gonna need some liquid courage to deal with more people like that man. As I took a few sips of whiskey, the red bastard appeared before my very eyes once again.

"What's wrong kid? You want to play in the big league's but you don't want to play big boy games? When did you become so morally righteous?" he said. I stood up and walked through Satan Nixon who disappeared like a cloud of smoke. I walked by a trashcan and threw away the flask, continuing to the next address on my list.

ACT II

"It's a big club and you ain't in it."
~GEORGE CARLIN, COMEDIAN, POSSIBLE TIME TRAVELER

CHAPTER 5

Everything Is Red

George Wallace was many things to many people, but a present father wasn't always one of them. He didn't do a great job at keeping secrets either. His ability to drink anyone under the table was unmatched and even going back to his time in college he enjoyed a good bar fight, a habit that didn't necessarily change as he got older. George's indiscrete affairs with numerous women were the talk of the town, and all these faults began to add up to the point where his loyal, yet passive wife Lurleen felt enough was enough.

Lurleen attempted to file for divorce on numerous occasions; she even had the support of her friends and family, but George always talked her out of it. That was George's ultimate power, gaslighting others and convincing them that his decisions were also theirs. His Luciferian silver tongue managed to keep others in line, a truly powerful trait in the arena of politics where you never knew if your friends and colleagues who hugged you in public one minute would stab you in the back the next. George wasn't above that behavior though; he knew how the game was played and played by the rules just as everyone else.

In their beautiful home, George and his family were sitting down at the dinner table. The maids were serving the Wallaces their plates of food while George was nursing a glass of whiskey on the rocks, observing his family. George would smile knowing that even though he wasn't what many would consider the father of the year, he provided his family with the blessings and privileges he never had as a child. For that reason, George was thankful.

Peggy, one of George's children, struck up a conversation regarding a class assignment about what each student thought was the most important thing in life. Lurleen smiled, "Family" she said to Peggy, "Family is the most important thing in life."

"Father what about you?" Peggy asked. George sat silently, taking a sip of his whiskey and a moment to look at everyone's face just once while he thought of what to say. One of the servants, who happened to be a black woman, was still in the room organizing utensils while they ate over a corner on stand-by should the Wallaces need anything else. He thought about whether he should say this in front of the help, but then realized he didn't even really care anymore what others thought. Everyone was benefitting from the fruits of his labor, who were they to judge him?

"Two things are most important in life," he said while looking back at Peggy, "Money and power, and I don't care for money." Lurleen didn't look at George or even consider saying anything, the whole froze and neither did Peggy or any of the others said anything. George finished his plate and his whiskey, stood up, and went back to his office without saying another word.

Gordon was a shit client, and I say that with all sincerity. I picked up more of a managerial role as the campaign progressed, leaving Colin with the task of organizing volunteers and trying to get some college friends to come out in exchange for whatever petty cash I could conjure up or the promise of free food. As Gordon predicted, as soon as he announced, one of his opponents did drop out, leaving the competition between him and Courtney Cole for the remainder of the primary. As soon as the final contestants became clear, Gordon must have mentally broken down because the rest of the race turned into a complete shit show.

Courtney was a short brunette, very nerdy with her secretarial looking glasses, but also cute at the same time. Looking at her you wouldn't have imagined that this thirty-something mother of two would turn out to be a complete Tupac when it came to playing the game. I've worked for many politicians and candidates, but that woman scares the living crap out of me to this day. In a weird sort of way, I kind of respect her for her tenacity. Not much was known about her; she kept a low profile in terms of the city government, but among Republican circles she was virtually unknown. There were rumors flying around that she was a closeted Democrat who was running as a Republican since the city and district as a whole were overwhelmingly Republican. Rumors are the sticks and stones of political ammunition, but Courtney was carrying straight nukes for the rest of the campaign.

"They quit" I told Gordon as we met up in a Wal-Mart parking lot to refill on door hangers.

"Why the fuck did they do that?" Gordon said. It was two weeks into the campaign and this dude wasn't shaving, ironing his suits, nor was he brushing his teeth. He was a complete and utter mess.

"Because you won't pay them more than a free lunch, and Courtney's paying them two dollars above minimum wage for the same work. What did you think was going happen in a Republican primary? People are gonna work for the Republican with money," I replied. "We have the resources Gordon, we can hire fifty door knockers to get every neighborhood in the county if we wanted to." He took out a cigarette and smoked while thinking of his next move. At this point the only people knocking on doors for him were Colin and me. I went over and smacked the cigarette out of his hand.

"What the hell was that for?" He said while reaching for his pack of smokes, more concerned with another cancer stick than anything else at the moment.

"You have to go talk to a classroom full of first graders this afternoon about the importance of elections and you smell like you've been bathing in menthols!" I replied.

"I'm not going to the school meet and whatever thingy," he said.

"What the Hell do you mean you aren't going to the school?" I replied, while holding my tongue so I didn't curse him out in public.

"First graders don't vote..." he said, just as I cut him off. I thought about pimp slapping him like it was going out of style, but with my luck this bastard and I would end up on YouTube because some brat with a phone would drive by and witness a latino man hitting a nice white fellow running for public office. No matter how angry I felt, the professional in me still screamed "optics."

"But their parents do! The people who read the newspaper and go online and see a photo of a politician being nice to kids do!" I yelled. "I will drag you to that elementary school myself if I have to."

"No, I'm going home to shower and get some sleep," Gordon replied while rubbing his face nervously.

"Best decision you made all day!" I turned around and got back into my car. I got on the road and immediately received a call from Colin. I knew if he was calling me instead of texting me there was a major problem.

"Jackson Short just said he won't be making an endorsement," Colin said.

"Why the fuck not Colin? Why on earth is he deciding not to make an endorsement now of all races?"

"I don't know..." Colin said, as I hung up on him midsentence. I was driving to Jackson's myself to get a clear answer. Jackson Short was the son of Alister Short, political heavyweight and auction tycoon. He was an only child, so needless to say he grew up rather comfortably. Jackson was a very loyal Republican but he had the nickname of "King Maker" since whomever he endorsed in the primaries usually ended up winning the party nomination at minimum. Only once in five years did one of his candidates not win a primary. Even then, Jackson stood side by side with the party nominee, smiling and shaking hands to let the world know a Republican was a Republican, and at the end of the day that was all that mattered.

I drove up to his mansion across town. Jackson was on his deck drinking a sweet tea dressed in a white suit like some plantation owner. As a twenty-something young man, the whole thing seemed out of place, but anyone who knew Jackson knew it was nothing out of the ordinary.

"Mr. Brown!" Jackson said, waving me over to come have a seat with him. "What a pleasure it is for you to stop by today!"

"Cut the shit Jackson, you're not endorsing anyone in this race and I find that to be unbelievable. What gives?" His wide smile disappeared, so did the pleasantries.

"I have my reasons and my reasons are my own. I don't have to do anything I don't want to," he said while sipping on his drink.

"Does Courtney have something on you?" I asked as his face turned from smug to angry real fast.

"She does" he replied, "there's no point in denying it as people have always spread rumors about me, but circumstances changed." Something clicked in my mind, I knew exactly what he was talking about.

Off to the side of the house was the swimming pool, and cleaning it today was a young latino man, conducting his duties shirtless as every few minutes he would glance over at us, lingering his gaze on Jackson. This situation was past rumors, now it was in the waters of blackmail.

"By circumstances, you mean evidence of something that would bring down your social score, huh, Jackson? Maybe something daddy wouldn't like brought up on the golf course?" I replied. He got mad and started getting red in the face. I didn't care if the guy was a closeted gay, what I cared about was that not endorsing Gordon meant certain death in this race, and for me that meant I'd be out of a job very soon.

"Don't insinuate anything from what I said," Jackson said sternly. Before he could continue, a soft voice from behind him spoke.

"Art! It's so lovely to see you!" The lovely siren sound called out. It was Vanessa Clair, in a yellow sundress that perfectly contrasted against her brown hair and blue eyes. Vanessa was a friend of mine from college. We dated for a bit but nothing came of it, which was mostly my doing. There was an obvious physical attraction as everyone around us knew, but she wanted a life of predictability and well, I've never been described as a predictable person. Vanessa came over and gave Jackson a kiss on the cheek. They started dating a few years ago. Together they were essentially Virginia royalty; Jackson's family was in politics and real estate, and Vanessa's family owned a large winery outside of Charlottesville. To outside observers, they seemed like a happy couple, but knowing a thing or two about Jackson, I knew all was not what it seemed.

"Hey Ness (the nickname I gave her in college) it's lovely to see you, but I was just about to leave." She pouted at me for a moment. I hadn't seen her in almost a year but looking at her again made my heart flutter. The last time we spoke to each other in person things weren't what anyone would consider pleasant. Months after the breakup she'd sent an email, I'd reply with a text maybe saying Merry Christmas or something, and after about a year or so we just stopped talking.

"Oh Art, we never see each other, but will you be at the debate tomorrow?" She asked. I had completely forgotten about it. The Republicans were holding their final gubernatorial primary debate at a few hours away at Liberty University a month before the primary. This was going to be a big deal, everyone who was anyone was going be there so they could woo and be wooed by the different candidates in a race that was too close to call.

"I will be, and I look forward to seeing you both there as well."

The next day Sabrina, Colin, and I were passing out campaign literature outside of the auditorium for Gordon at the debate. There were easily a thousand or more people in attendance. State Senator Frank Wagner, lobbyist and heir-apparent to the nomination Ed Gillespie, and Prince William County Board of Supervisors Chairman Corey Stewart were here tonight to spar in person for the last time. No one assumed Frank was a serious competitor, he was at single digits in the polls. The real race was between Ed Gillespie and Corey Stewart. Gillespie, who had lost the 2014 senate race, was still treated as Republican royalty since the establishment Republicans loved him, and there was a myth going around he appealed to moderates and independents in Northern Virginia. Corey Stewart was interesting; he was for the longest time seen as the future of the Virginia GOP, having won numerous re-elections in a blue county and nearly clinching enough delegates at the state convention for the 2013 Lt. Governor's nomination.

In 2016, however, Corey set his gaze on higher aspirations. As chairman of the Virginia Trump campaign, he led a rally at the Republican National Committee who he was accusing of trying to sabotage Trump in the primaries. Trump repaid Corey by firing him the next day, but that was enough to give Corey a populist following who were willing to give their time, and their money. In 2017, moderate, nice guy Corey (born and raised in Minnesota) rebranded himself as a southern populist with a grudge against "the Yankees." He forced hardline stances on immigration and the protection of Confederate monuments on all the Republicans down ballot, even bringing Gillespie to go on the record about topics he obviously didn't want to. It was a strange move for anyone that knew anything about Corey, but it was enough for him to give the Establishment's chosen one, Ed Gillespie, a run for his money.

Sabrina was wearing a blue skirt with red heels, colors which complimented her bleached blonde hair perfectly. She was not a political person in the slightest, but she always came out to help when I needed it. Shorthanded that day since Gordon refused to incentivize workers and volunteers, she came without a second's hesitation. A local city councilman came by and was quickly captivated by Sabrina. I saw from a distance as she smiled and passed him one of Gordon's flyers. He awkwardly stood there for a moment as she held her arm out waiting for him to take the flyer but he obviously was looking directly at her cleavage. He took a flyer after eyeing her from head to toe and walked off, tossing the flyer into a trash bin when he was far enough away to not seem rude.

Sabrina was accustomed to men objectifying her, but she also knew that she would become the guilty one if she caused a scene by calling out the councilman. She was a stronger woman than people gave her credit for. We continued passing out flyers until the debate started.

After the debate ended, there was a reception held in the lobby where the Republican elite drank and laughed as if the three campaigns all of a sudden became friends. As soon as those people went home they'd all be texting each other terrible remarks about other people, but for now they drank and smiled. Sabrina wanted to get a picture with Ed Gillespie, who was greeting some local volunteers in a room off to the side of the lobby. As she walked towards the door, a horde of male volunteers quickly rushed out so they could get some food and managed to knock her over. I was in the bathroom at the time texting Gordon trying to find out why he wasn't at the debate. As Sabrina struggled to get up, she saw Ed Gillespie and his manager walk out, look at her on the floor, and keep walking. Not a single person walking out of that room helped her up or came over to see if she was alright.

"May I help you ma'am?" Said the man standing behind her as he reached his arm out across her right shoulder.

"Thank you sir," she said as he helped her up.

"It's alright, I'm glad to be of service" he said smiling. The man was Malin, one of the Congressman's primary staff from the campaign. I walked out and saw Sabrina was very clearly upset as she walked over to me.

"Is everything alright?" I asked.

"Yeah, everything is fine, I'm gonna head home since it's getting late." She kissed me and walked off. She was too strong and proud of a woman to tell me what was bothering her as we were there. Gordon showed up in the same wrinkled suit from the day before, a freaking embarrassment who smelled like cheap booze. I saw him walking towards me with Malin right beside him.

"Art, you know Malin right?" Gordon asked.

"Yeah we worked on the same campaign together" I said, shaking Malin's hand. Colin walked over to us with a plate of cake, obviously having given up passing out campaign flyers. Malin lit up as Colin walked over.

"Colin! My man!" Malin said as the two of them started some funky fist bump, shoulder slap secret handshake. I had no clue that the two of them really knew each other, nonetheless have some members-only hand shake. Gordon had a strange smile across his face, which was odd since I'd never seen him smile.

"Malin is taking some time off from the Congressman's office to come down and help us out a bit," Gordon said to me.

"I didn't know you were working full time in D.C. right now," I said to Malin.

"I got hired about a week ago in the legislative shop," he replied. Strange, it seems like everyone was getting hired in an office that wasn't hiring anyone. Gordon got between us and slapped each of us on the back.

"I think we need a clear direction to success," Gordon said in a condescending tone that oozed a cocky arrogance I couldn't stand.

"Like show up to events on time and shower? Maybe pay the kids that are running over to Courtney," I replied. Gordon didn't find that remark funny at all as his smile disappeared.

"After looking at your progress, or lack of progress," Malin said, beginning to irritate me further, "I think we need to take more of an aggressive route against Courtney going forward." I don't know what Gordon and Malin had been talking about but we obviously weren't working in the same plane of reality.

"It's time we start going after the fact she's obviously a liberal trying to steal the Republican nomination," Malin said to me.

"Don't attack what you're not willing to kill, dude. You strike first, all bets are off, and she seems to have more going for her thanks to her family's wealth than sparky here who refuses to hit up the dry cleaners," I said, gesturing to Gordon's unkempt appearance.

"With all respect Art, I've ran enough races to know when to start getting aggressive," said Malin.

I looked over his shoulder and saw Satan Nixon tipping a glass of wine my way with that sinister smile of his. This wasn't gonna end well.

I don't like playing dirty, because once you do, you tend to lose any sense of control over the situation you might think you have. George Wallace realized if he was going to get into the bull ring, he might as well be the bull instead of the rider hanging on for dear life. In politics, you don't have friends; you only have enemies you're dealing with now and enemies you're dealing with later. Much like a bull in a state of full on rage, George saw everyone and everything as a shade of red.

The first rider to step into the arena with the newer, more relentless George was a close friend of his from college. Frank Johnson, a respected and talented attorney who graduated from the University of Alabama the same year as George. While Johnson wasn't a boxer, George respected his ferocity and cunning in the courtroom, much like he would a skilled opponent in the ring. It made perfect sense that Frank Johnson would grow up to become a federal judge one day.

In 1959, George forced Frank into the ring. The federal government, while still divided on the specifics of any substantial civil rights legislation, was marching towards the Jim Crow states blazing a Sherman-like path that couldn't be stopped. George realized he could rebrand himself by fighting the federal government in the cradle of the Confederacy. The federal government issued an order asking the state of Alabama to comply by turning over voting records to an investigation regarding vote tampering and voter suppression.

"You want me to do what?" Frank Johnson, surprised as all hell, asked George, hoping that somehow he misheard what George had just asked of him.

"I'll refuse to comply with the federal order and you just have to give me a slap on the hand by placing me in jail for a night or so. This isn't a fight we can win but it is a fight we can showboat around to make a point or two," George said while sitting across from Frank in Johnson's office. George continued puffing on his cigar while Frank paused to fully comprehend what he had just heard.

"You want to go to jail?" Frank asked.

"I want them to know they are stepping on the sovereignty of the state of Alabama in order to corner us into a situation where we're gonna lose control over," George replied. Frank paused for another moment as a look of disgust spread across his face.

"This has nothing to do with the blacks or with the law at all George, and you know it," Frank said sternly. Wallace didn't flinch or bat an eye; he just kept puffing on his cigar. Frank chose his side, and now George was gonna have to throw the first punch.

Wallace didn't end up going to jail, but he refused to comply in his role as a circuit judge long enough to capture national attention as being the lone judge to try and block the progress of the federal investigation. This was a strange defeat because Wallace knew the whole time he wasn't going to block the feds for long, but that wasn't the point. Wallace knew that in this match, the goal wasn't necessarily to knock out Frank Johnson; it was to go as many rounds as possible, and in essence, show the pro-segregationist south every punch he was taking, he was taking for them. Wallace may have been defeated in a court of law, but in the court of public opinion he was the people's champion.

After that whole situation, Frank Johnson and George Wallace never spoke again. Years later, however, Wallace would have a thing or two to say about his old friend Judge Johnson, calling him at rally after rally a "bald faced, carpetbagging, scally-wagging, integrating liar."

CHAPTER 6

Bad Jack

A few days before Colin and I met with Gordon at Waffle House, I had received a call from an old colleague of mine, Max Getty. Max was by far the most effective campaign manager I had ever seen in action, and in terms of political moxy, Max was a miracle worker. Max heard I was in the market for a new client, so he called me to see if I would want to work for Courtney Cole at a reduced rate, with the incentive that, Courtney would easily win the Republican nomination, and then I could be brought on as the full time campaign manager for the general election after the primary.

"Why are you involved in her race, Max? You've been with the local GOP committee for years and no one has ever heard of this chick," I asked.

"Her father and I go way back, they are good folk," he replied. I thought it over, but the thing was I wasn't going to take a reduced rate for an unknown candidate when I knew I could get a ton of cash upfront from Gordon.

"Sorry, Max, but looks like I'll be taking on Gordon Pecker for this go around." I could hear him sighing over the phone.

"Well, that's a shame to hear buddy," he said. "Bad Jack is bad news my man." Little did I know then how right Max was.

Gordon Pecker was many things, but he was not going to be the city's next Treasurer, that was almost certain. Under Malin's guidance, they ran a ton of commercials calling him a hardworking family man, and Courtney Cole a closeted liberal who would bankrupt the city if Republicans didn't wise up and vote for Gordon in the upcoming primary. Malin convinced Gordon to throw the first punch and by drawing first blood, gave Courtney's team a blank check to do whatever they wanted as long as it hurt Gordon.

A week after the gubernatorial debate, photos of Pecker in the backseat of his car with his best friend's wife were sent to his house. Unlucky for Gordon, his wife found the photos first. Even worse, his wife got a hold of his cell phone records, and found that for over a year, right around the time she had given birth to their second child, he had been flirting and sending inappropriate messages to this other woman. A few days before Gordon's campaign launch, the affair went from textual to sexual. Now I had worked for many candidates before Gordon and I had witnessed many stupid things, but having his wife as the admin on his campaign Facebook page while cheating on her was the dumbest thing I had ever witnessed.

Lisa Pecker, Gordon's wife, posted the photos and the screenshots of the text messages onto the campaign page, kicked off Gordon and everyone else who had admin access, and grabbed the kids so they could stay at her parent's house for the time being. Gordon was a laughing stock in the media and online. As acting vice president of the local Tea Party, he was asked to step down for "flawed and exposed lack of character." Malin saw this incident and tried to shrug it off as if it wasn't a big deal. Under the smug confidence, he was sweating bullets.

"Plenty of people have affairs, believe me," he said on local radio, which already showed how bad things had gotten when the campaign manager had to go do damage control instead of the candidate. "The voters are selecting a proven and conservative steward of their taxpayer dollars, not a saint." The host sitting across from Malin in the studio pulled out some printed articles.

"But recent documents showed that Mr. Pecker spent $3,000 on a video game called Fortnite, how is that responsible?" The host asked. Malin was screwed, even he couldn't find a way to spin that.

"That's just another lie about a good man being spread by liberal Courtney Cole."

"But these documents were provided to the local paper by Lisa Pecker..." the host said before Malin slammed his fist on the table.

"Lisa Pecker is a schizophrenic bitch!" Malin screamed for all the listeners at home to hear.

The champagne was popped. Courtney Cole had the election in the bag from that point on. Malin texted me hundreds of times talking about new strategies and alternative options. I blocked his number and Gordon's too, instead sending an email that said "contract terminated." Primary day came and went, and instead of working all day and night like I had every primary and general election day prior, I stayed home in my boxers, eating Ben and Jerry's ice cream out of the tub with a bottle of Jim Beam while watching repeats of *The Office* on TV.

Corey Stewart lost the Republican nomination to Ed Gillespie by less than 1%, an outcome no one saw coming as Ed got all the endorsements and outspent Corey like it was going out of style. Corey's election night party felt more like a victory party than Ed's did. The fact that Gillespie had almost lost to mini-Trump Corey meant the odds of him carrying them to victory against Democrat Ralph Northam in November was slim to none. That night, most of Ed's donors went cold turkey and a number of his staff quit so they could find a job on a winning campaign. Corey, on the other hand, was smiling and celebrating the close call with supporters. "This isn't the end," he said to the crowd, several weeks later announcing his bid for US Senate. Maybe Corey knew the entire time he couldn't knockout Ed in the ring, but once again everyone watched him go round after round with the man who was supposed to take him out with one punch.

As for Gordon's race, he lost to Courtney Cole by a 30 percent margin. I watched the local news on TV report from her victory party, where Jackson Short was standing behind a podium with her name on the placard, introducing to the crowd the Republican nominee for Treasurer of our proud city. I laughed to myself. I mean, how much of a coward do you have to be to go out and smile and sing the praises of someone holding blackmail over your head? Maybe it wasn't even fear, maybe Courtney and Jackson saw a little bit of themselves in each other; after all, game respects game.

I got a call from Vanessa a few minutes after the final numbers came in. "I'm sorry Art, but I couldn't convince myself to go out and vote for your candidate this time around."

"That's alright," I told her, "I couldn't either."

I fell asleep, still in my boxers on the couch after finishing all the ice cream and half the bottle. For a moment, I actually felt at peace with the world. I quit that shitshow with just enough time to say I had no responsibility for what that pig did if he actually managed to get elected. If anything, I think Courtney owed me a thank you, since most of my friends either didn't vote at all or decided to swing their votes for her after I left.

"Hey there, pal," an echoing voice bouncing off the walls of my apartment said as I felt a finger tapping on my head. It was Satan Nixon, the demon in the bottle that came with every shot of Jim Beam. "Wanna hear a bedtime story?"

I opened my eyes and saw him wearing my bathrobe, sitting on my reclining chair next to my couch holding a large leather bound book. I was about to tell him to go take a hike, but he snapped his fingers causing my mouth to disappear from my face. I began to freak out but I knew this was just an alcohol fueled dream, and it would all be over soon. Just had to breath and ride it out, just like a panic attack.

"This one is a real doozy baby. It's called *The Seven Deadly Dwarves*." He opened the book and suddenly a blast of fire erupted under my coffee table bursting through it. "Once upon a time in a boggy swamp, there was a gal named Snow White who was running for queen of the kingdom, and she needed some help from the seven deadly dwarves." All of a sudden the sound of laughter began to fill of the room, as if a crowd of children were hiding somewhere.

"First there was Sleazy, a dwarf who would work for anyone who paid," Satan Nixon said. Out of the fire jumped out a dwarf in a little suit with a face that looked like Bill Clinton's advisor James Carville, wearing the iconic glasses and bald head matching that that essential cajun sneer. "Then there was Slutty who will do anything to get ahead, and I mean literally anything." Up from the fire popped out a female dwarf dressed like a Vegas stripper, who then jumped onto Satan Nixon's lap. "But we can't forget the rest of the team! Sinister, the dwarf with no ethical boundaries! Sadist, the dwarf who loves to hurt others! Sadness, who can steal the hopes of the masses and fill them with depression! Savvy, the dwarf who can sell porn to a nun and convince smart people to buy Enron stock! And Successful, the dwarf who can throw a real winner of a party!" All those little demonic midgets were running around the apartment, drinking my booze and prank calling people on my cell phone. At one point one of them went to my TV and started buying every movie on-demand.

"Is this some type of twisted subconscious lesson I'm supposed to learn?" I said as my mouth began to reappear on my face. "I quit the bastard's race, I chose to stay away from it all."

"Oh pal, oh pal o'mine, I'm not here to teach you a lesson. I'm here to show my friends a good time and what a loser looks like!" Satan Nixon began laughing again as Slutty came over and lit a fresh cigar for him. "This is the company you keep, Art. You make a good decision once and you think that makes you a good person in the long run? You were pimping out that shitshow until you couldn't contain it anymore. You promoted that walking, talking, piece of filth around town knowing you couldn't trust him to feed your dog, but you tried to convince others he could cure cancer and feed the poor." He came over and pressed his cigar into my chest. I screamed like I had never screamed before as the ashes stuck to the wound.

"Our actions have consequences, buddy boy!" The dwarfs started laughing even louder than before. "The funniest part of it is you bugged out and you're still as much of a loser now than you were prior! You wouldn't even go down with the ship! You just left everyone to drown! Think of how Gordon's little kids are gonna see their daddy as they get older, a man who shouldn't have been running but you just kept moving along with it all." Suddenly two of the dwarfs grabbed me by the feet as Sadist and Sinister held down my legs while Sleazy and Successful sat on each of my arms. Sinister and Sadness pulled out some baseball bats and started beating me, while Slutty grabbed some bottles of vodka and a funnel and started drowning me as I slipped into unconsciousness. "It pays to be a winner!" Satan Nixon yelled out as the dwarfs began to chant it over and over again until the whole room went black.

My eyes eventually peeled back open as I began to regain consciousness. I felt like I was thrown into a cold lake, but as I looked around my blurred surroundings, I saw that I had emptied out all the ice from my freezer and dumped it into my bathtub, where at some point I decided to step inside. I must have had some animal instinct take over as my body was in a drunken survival mode. Everything was doubled, my vision came in and out every few seconds as I struggled to crawl out of the tub. I kept thinking to myself I should have never signed on Gordon as a client; he only brought disappointment to those around him and a trashed reputation for me. I knew I couldn't have stopped him from making self-destructive decisions, but I didn't ruin his marriage or bring on that slick serpent Malin. Still, maybe I could have been more vocal early on, actually paid attention and shed light on the red flags in his behavior so, I could have pushed him in a better direction, or at least been proactive in clearing any guilt that would lay on my mind later.

On the floor next to the toilet, I saw my iPhone screen glowing. I missed another call from Vanessa, three texts from Sabrina, a Tweet from Colin, and a long email from the Congressman's personal email. I was too hungover to read and reply, so I slowly dried up with a towel so I could go to the kitchen and get some food. I still didn't know what time it was or how long I was out. Was I really hungover, or was I still drunk? Was it even the same day? Nothing made sense as I was just trying to function second to second without blacking out all over again. I saw half a bottle of beer on the counter, mistaking it for a bottle of water so I chugged it while ignoring the clear taste that screamed this was anything but water.

I looked over at my analogue wall clock hoping to get a grasp of what time it was, but both hands were rotating out of control as if the thing needed an exorcism. The whole apartment was still dark, which made everything worse as I felt more light-headed by the minute. I knew I kept a bottle of caffeine pills in my suitcase, so I got back on my stomach and crawled across the kitchen floor. Walking on two feet with some sense of coordination in that moment was like asking me to fly. My body fluctuated between hot and cold, and the only thing going well in that situation was that my body was perspiring enough to help me glide across the linoleum floor from my kitchen to my suitcase near the door.

The suitcase was open, but I was hit with another challenge. There were three to four pill bottles, and like everything else I couldn't read what was on the labels. There was only one rational decision to make in this alcohol induced state- swallow one pill from every bottle. Slowly as the pills kicked in I began to realize while one of them was definitely a caffeine pill, one was migraine medication, and the other was a sleeping pill. There wasn't much of an opportunity to freak out about the fact I took three aggressive medications with enough alcohol flowing through my veins to cover a hotel room party at CPAC. I was already starting to feel my limbs go numb as my chest tightened, and it became more difficult to stay awake.

What a shitty way to die; naked on your floor covered with bottles of pills while smelling like a wet dog. As the universe would have it, I wouldn't die that moment. My eyes opened up once again what I felt was only several hours later. I turned my head near my couch and saw a shirtless man smoking a cigarette while cleaning what seemed to be a pistol. I didn't want to say anything; it could have been a home invader or an hallucination. Still, if this person was there, maybe he'd at least get me to an emergency room so a responsible adult could make decisions for me instead of me, an obvious failure, making one for myself in that moment.

"Hey man, are you really there?" I asked the mysterious figure. He didn't reply, but after I spoke I heard the laughter of the damned seven deadly dwarfs once again echoing throughout the room. "Satan...Nixon...Satan Nixon...Nixon" I kept rattling that name hoping if it was my hallucinatory devil, at least he'd talk back.

"The inevitable question, which of course, everybody asks is, do I really carry two weapons in my hands and hold them throughout every love making session?" The mysterious figure said, as if we were in the middle of some strange conversation already. "Yes, and I always have" the man's raspy voice said. I was stunned, not just by the most random sentence I had ever heard in my life but who the hallucination manifested itself to be- tech pioneer, accused murderer, and former Libertarian presidential candidate John McAfee. Months ago during the 2016 election, he had called me after receiving my number from a friend and asked if I'd be willing to run his campaign in exchange for hookers, drugs, guns, and Bitcoin. Obviously, I said no, but that memory stuck. He stood up from the couch and turned around to face me. "Why?" He asked as he looked down at me.

"I don't know, I literally didn't ask you anything ever," I replied.

"It's because I have survived thirty-one home invasions in my seventy-three years, and these invasions were not normal street pimps and people, they were usually special forces soldiers, and why?" he asked again.

"Dude, I'm literally not even saying anything, but you keep asking me like I am," I said while reaching for a gym towel to cover myself up.

"Because I'm a special mother fucker." I blinked and suddenly I was standing, fully clothed in my work blazer and college sweatpants, holding a gun in my right hand with an apple on my head as John McAfee stood right across from me, holding a gun with an apple atop his head. "Now hit the apple," said McAfee, shirtless exposing his Maori tattoo with the residue of cocaine on his nose.

"John, there is no way in hell I'm shooting," I said.

"Do it bud-o, do it for the audience!" I heard Satan Nixon yell out from behind me. He was standing in my kitchen all excited with the dwarfs chanting "Shoot him in the head! Shoot him in the head!" I aimed the gun at the apple, fired, and the fruit burst apart in slow motion.

"My turn" McAfee said, this time shooting me directly in the forehead. I didn't "die" immediately, but I fell back in slow motion for what felt like forever. I saw glimpses of my life flash before my eyes. I saw all the campaigns I volunteered on as a kid. I saw all the long nights I spent making signs for candidates and getting ready to drive to rallies. I saw every bitter defeat, and every small victory my team and I achieved. I saw the Congressman slap me on the back with pride, but then I saw all the nights I chose to plot and plan instead of spending time with Sabrina. I saw every lie and every cheap shot I said to harm an opponent. I saw every backroom deal I made to secure a contract and every person who stabbed me in the back. Then, like a snap of the fingers, lights out, ka-boom.

Two days later, I was still nursing the most killer headache of my life in what felt like a constant hangover. I went to a french cafe in Alexandria to meet Dwayne for breakfast. He was doing well, attending Georgetown parties and taking selfies with the powerful elite. By the end of his first month, he'd already slept with most the young, college aged interns in the office. I hated him for getting a job I'd kill for, but I was just happy he was happy; it was a strange combination of feelings I couldn't express fully into words.

"Man, I hate to ask you for a favor, but I messed up big time recently," Dwayne said. I was really hoping he wasn't going to ask for money, I was down to the last $200 in cash I stored in my wallet until I could sign another candidate. "I did something recently which currently froze my checking and savings accounts." I rubbed my eyes, knowing I was either gonna hurt financially, personally, or let down a friend in need.

"What did you do, Dwayne?" I asked. He sipped his coffee while looking around the cafe in case he saw someone he knew.

"You know how on most mobile banking apps you can deposit a check by just taking a photo of it?" He said, "I printed some fake checks off the internet and deposited them." I was dumbfounded, stealing was bad enough but signing your own checks to yourself, that was the most retarded thing I'd ever heard. "The bank isn't gonna call the feds, but they cancelled my account with them and they are sending me a check with my remaining money, which may take one to two weeks. I didn't wanna ask for money Art, but I just pawned my laptop the other day and I can't get an advance at work."

I was sad for his misfortune but also disgusted by his lack of character. What else was I supposed to do though? Dwayne and I were close friends, and he needed me. I pulled out a hundred-dollar bill from my wallet and passed it to him. Later, I'd go buy back his laptop without telling him I was doing so and mail it to his office in D.C. Dwayne made a mistake, but I thought this would help put him on the right track.

Dwayne left for work but I decided to stay and order another coffee. Refills were free and I was unemployed for the foreseeable future so I was smart enough to take advantage of a good thing. I hoped Dwayne really did learn from his mistakes, but for now I needed to remain optimistic for his sake and mine.

I realized now would be a good time to respond to all calls, texts, and emails I had gotten from a few days prior. The Congressman's email was short.

"Art, heard that last candidate of yours was a flame-out, real bummer, but we all have that one campaign we don't put on our resume. Anyway, long story short, Bart Keller is out as chief of staff, I'm gonna find you a place in the office if you want but you'll have to wait, the new Chief of Staff is cleaning house to bring in some new blood." The next part of the email made my blood run cold. "You remember Malin? He'll be taking over as chief of staff..."

"I don't know about this fella," George said to Trammell as he put out his cigar in the ashtray on the table. George and Seymour were sitting at a table at a BBQ joint in Tuscaloosa, where Seymour Trammell arranged a meeting with a man who would help George build inroads with the hardline segregationists he lost five years ago. "His is a politics that is gonna distract a lot of people from the point I'm trying to make."

"George," Seymour patted George's hand, "you can't make things better if you aren't making the laws." A tall man of wide girth and a rather large forehead walked over to the table, smiling at both men.

"Gentlemen, I'm Asa Carter" he said, shaking both men's hands. He made eye contact with George, "and I'm here to make you governor." George smiled back, knowing if he wanted to win this campaign, he was going to have to understand that shaking Carter's hand was a Faustian bargain from which he wouldn't get to simply walk away.

George decided in 1962 to run once again for the Democratic nomination for governor. This time things would be different; this time he was going to play like Patterson played last time- dirty. In the state of Alabama, the state constitution didn't allow the governor to serve two consecutive terms. Patterson was out, meaning George, who had now reached folk hero status for his stand against Judge Frank Johnson and the federal government several years prior, had a favorable lead over the field of Democrats who were running. Wallace's main opponent was his friend and mentor Jim Folsom, who was also the governor of Alabama while George was still in the state house. Folsom was a popular governor, showing young George how to play the game of politics in order to get your policy and turn it into reality. Folsom always felt Wallace's progressive views were ahead of his time and knew one day George would be able to be a changemaker, if he so chose. The 1962 race for governor showed Folsom that the man he once knew had changed, but not for the better. As Obi-Wan Kenobi had raised Anakin Skywalker into manhood, so had Folsom raised Wallace. However, just like the two Jedi, Wallace would strike down his former mentor and friend, giving into the dark side.

Asa Carter was brought onto the campaign in order to do one thing, brand Wallace as the candidate of segregationists and white supremacists. A former Ku Klux Klan grand wizard, Asa Carter was known in the underground of the white nationalist movement as a true radical. Wallace knew that unlike Patterson, who was always speaking of segregation and racial politics, he couldn't hide his past as a moderate Democrat who was once endorsed by the NAACP. Wallace needed Carter's advice and credibility if he was to tap into the spurred white voters who felt the civil rights movement was a threat to their life. Schools and jobs be damned, George was going to give the voters bread and circuses.

Rally after rally, George attacked Frank Johnson over and over. Reminding everyone of the scalps he was willing to collect if it meant Alabama was free of federal interference. Additionally, he called the civil rights protestors and activists throughout the country communists, as well as painting his opponents, Jim Folsom included, as weak men would fold to pressure from Washington D.C. as the civil rights movement moved closer to success each and every day. Wallace obtained a commanding lead once the campaign started, but the night belonged to Asa Carter, who traveled to KKK and other pro-segregationist groups to let them know that if they wanted someone who sympathized with their cause to go represent them in Montgomery, George Wallace was that candidate.

Wallace destroyed Folsom and his other opponents on primary day, showing the politics of poverty relief and infrastructure couldn't cut it in a race dictated by segregation. The era of folks like lovable Jim Folsom were over, and the time now belonged to a darkened, ruthless George Wallace, who would win the general election months later, finally reaching his goal of becoming governor of Alabama.

On January 14, 1963, Asa Carter delivered on his promise to the Klan and pro-segregationists to put a sympathizer in the governorship. Carter spent week's prepping on Wallace's speech, knowing this would leave a mark on history that would define not only racial politics in America, but also the legacy of Wallace. An immense crowd of supporters and press gathered as Wallace was inaugurated as governor. Soon enough, he walked up to the podium to issue a declaration which would define who George Wallace was in the eyes of American history forever. "In the name of the greatest people that have ever trod this earth, I draw the line in the dust and toss the gauntlet before the feet of tyranny, and I say segregation now, segregation tomorrow, segregation forever."

It was July, and I was out of a job. Sabrina begged me not to get involved with the 2017 election. By that point she had also explained to me how she had been pushed and disrespected by Ed Gillespie and his posse. Something in her gut told her I needed to stay out of this race, and lucky for her, no one was hiring so I didn't have much of a choice. I had one opportunity, however, to work for a Super PAC supporting Gillespie. I was tied, asking myself if I should take a job working on behalf of the man who looked my girlfriend square in the eyes as she was down on the floor and continued walking, or just accept that I wasn't going to get a paycheck for a while because I felt Sabrina didn't want me to? I resented everyone, I just wanted everything to work my way.

I got a call from Colin, who was on summer break preparing to start his final semester in school. He told me how he was now working for Corey Stewart's senate campaign, but something was bothering him and making him consider quitting. Corey had hired several key staffers of former Wisconsin Republican congressional candidate Paul Nehlen. That was all Colin had to tell me for a gut wrenching feeling to form right in my stomach. Nehlen was an open, proud white supremacist who wanted to stick Jews in concentration camps along with other despicable ideas. For Corey, who had already during the primary for governor called Ed Gillespie a "cuckservative" and made up conspiracies of Ed being responsible for human trafficking during his time as a consultant at Tyson's Chicken, to now hire two men who helped run the race for Nehlen, showed the type of company he chose to keep. Corey, who many conservatives had forgiven for certain antics in the 2017 race for governor, showed he was willing to say and do anything to win while at the same time losing many of the people who had his back.

"I've got a feeling in my gut that these guys are gaslighting folks. I don't know what to make of it because it seems like they're not as much interested in campaigning as they are going out and pulling political stunts. The staff aren't what I would consider friendly towards volunteers and potential supporters," Colin told me over the phone. I paused for a moment as I thought of my next words carefully.

"Colin, you're your own man. You've gotta determine if this is what you want to surround yourself with," I replied.

On August 12th, 2017, the Charlottesville riot occurred. Colin quit immediately after several of Corey's close friends and staff were seen rallying arm in arm with white supremacists.

CHAPTER 7

Man on Fire

I t was the day after Election Day 2013 in Virginia. The night prior, Max Getty and I were shit-faced at a bar in Reston where we saw the Democrats narrowly take the governorship from us, along with the contested Attorney General and Lt. Governor's slot. Max was my boss during that race. I was just a lowly intern, but he took an interest in me and made me his aide for the district we were responsible for canvassing on behalf of the Republican gubernatorial candidate, former Attorney General Ken Cuccinelli.

"You'd think after Romney's fumbling, Republicans would turn out for a real conservative. Now, in about four or five months they'll be parading someone like that pussy Ed Gillespie around for Senate by complaining that Cuccinelli is too right wing and too scary for mushy moderates that want to go about their days thinking everything is fine because nobody is rocking the boat," Max said, before taking his seventh shot of tequila. "Freaking sheep, all of those so called moderates who voted for Terry because he seemed like a nice guy, someone you can be seen virtue signaling at a cocktail party with so you can grandstand amongst your friends and neighbors." Max was principled and vitriolic back in those days, especially when Ron Paul was running for president in 2008 and 2012. Six months later he'd become a consultant for Gillespie's senate run, and three years later consult for his general election campaign, as well. I guess Max hitched himself to the guy who paid the most, because everyone knows the best person for the job isn't always the one that ends up getting it. Voters don't care about credibility, they care about everything but credibility. We settled the tab and went our separate ways that evening. That'd be the last time I'd talk to Max until he tried to warn me about Gordon Pecker years later. "What are you gonna do now kid?" he asked me.

"Go back to delivering pizzas until I can find the next fight," I said. Max chuckled as he slapped me on the back.

"A Georgetown grad delivering pizzas," he said while trying to contain his laughter, "how did my generation screw yours up so badly?"

I honestly thought Cuccinelli would have won that day, but there was something in my gut that told me he was gonna lose. It was as if I had some electoral sixth sense in my mind telling me to brace for impact. It was the same feeling I had the day before the presidential election in 2012, seeing the Romney team in Virginia pull out all the stops knowing in the last days, no undecided voter really existed. I woke up the next day, the same way I had felt days prior, feeling nothing at all about the American   body   politic. Pundits try and tell you what the American people want but it's never what they are really saying. In fact, they're more honest than they receive credit for, because at the end of the day only the talking heads and pundits actually end up surprised with the results. You can glean more knowledge from a trucker and a gas station owner about how the American people think than listening to a man on cable TV wearing a bespoke suit. This, like many other things, is a lesson you only learn after you've been burned out and discarded from the political scene, like a ghost watching the living make the same mistakes over and over, screaming the truth even though no one can hear you.

I decided to stick around after finishing college and remain living in Georgetown. The studio I was living in wasn't in the type of shape you'd expect for the Georgetown prices I was paying. After all you're paying for location, not quality. There was a dark, wide stretch of water damage on my ceiling and water from the night's rain began to break through the thin layer keeping it together as it dripped straight down into my bed. That morning, the water droplets didn't wake me up; they woke up Vanessa who was sleeping on my right side while wearing my Romney/Ryan 2012 t-shirt.

"I hate rain," she said while her face was pressed firmly into her pillow. "I hate it like voters hate making reasonable decisions." I laughed and got up to get a towel. She turned over and stretched out to grab me as I returned to the bed, shimmying over to my side as I laid the towel down. "What are you doing today?" She asked me, as I laid back down and she rested her head on my chest. The smell of her brown hair was like honey. I took a moment just to breathe it in before thinking of how to answer back.

"I think I'm gonna ask Max if he can link me up with a few of the big senate races in the midwest or down south, and see if maybe we can get a win out there and flip a few seats," I said. Vanessa, who felt loose and relaxed a moment ago, suddenly got stiff; I knew that wasn't what she wanted to hear at all. The last few months I was focused on the campaign entirely while she was focusing on what our lives could be together after the election. Win or lose, after the race was run she wanted to become my next priority, but deep down even I realized that was something I couldn't give her, and it was only a matter of time until she was going to have to know that's how I felt about things. It's not that I didn't love her, but I didn't love her enough for what she deserved.

"You've done so much for so little for so many ungrateful people, Art. When are you going to make yourself a priority?" She asked me, lifting her chin on my chest and looking me straight in the eyes.

"I've gotta put in my all, Ness; I'm doing this for our country." My lackluster play for patriotism points didn't smooth things over or romance her in any way. I could tell that was not what she wanted to hear come out of my mouth. All through college all I did was focus on campus politics and jumping between races in Maryland and Virginia, while Vanessa was rightfully focusing on her grades. I told her I was setting myself up for something big, long before we started actually dating. My mistake our senior year was thinking I could balance paying attention to her and paying attention to working for candidates that didn't even know my name, despite being in their face constantly. After we graduated, I could tell she thought that time for me to focus on us was finally coming, except I'd just keep moving the goalposts further and further away, turning days into weeks and weeks into months.

"If you go off to Indiana or Kansas or some other state far away from here for a few months or maybe a year, what am I supposed to do? Do you just want me to go about my life waiting for you to come back so I can pretend you choosing to go far away for some campaign that's probably going to make you work twenty-four hours a day for no pay is alright with me? When you know I want you here so we can build our futures together?" She said, holding back tears as she realized we were finally having *that* conversation.

"It's not about that, Ness," I said. That was probably the first lie I ever intentionally told her. It was about *that*, everything was about that, fulfilling some fantasy that I could change the entire country by working for one candidate or just winning one campaign somewhere, and thinking all that would mean something grander than what it really was. I was caught up in the lie that each election was dictated by God, and each man or woman was ordained to fulfill some righteous path on behalf of their communities; meaning the losers were cast out from grace, and the winners had a charter from the heavens to rule as they pleased. It was just a game at the end of the day - a game devised by flawed men in which only fools would think it was anything more than that.

"When are you going to be satisfied, Art? Because obviously I'm not enough for you." We barely talked for the rest of the day, and for the next several days we only made eye contact on a couple occasions. We both knew my mind was made up. How could I love her when I didn't even really love myself? I was in love with an idea that if I could find something grand to be a part of, maybe I could love the purpose which I was granted, thus have an excuse from those around me to accept maybe I was good enough. All those years I lost, struggled, delivered pizzas to pay for school, suddenly I would be someone important in the eyes of other people, ignoring the fact that Ness already loved me for who I was. Later that week, I moved to Oklahoma for work, and wouldn't see Ness for four years.

In politics, many hundreds of young, fresh-faced (and some not so fresh faced) freshman legislators ranging from state houses to Washington D.C., all expect their *Mr. Smith Goes to Washington* moment to define their legacies as champions for the people. Instead, they trade in their principles for convenient reservations at fancy restaurants and invitations to parties. More often than not, ranging from fiscal hawk Republicans to civil libertarian Democrats, the idealists at one point or another all get "rolled."

In 2018, outgoing Florida Congressman Tom Rooney sat down with a reporter from *Vice News* to discuss his biggest regrets during his time in the House of Representatives. "I got rolled," he explained, discussing how he came to Washington expecting to vote against debt ceiling increases and increased deficit spending, only to end up getting "rolled" and voting for bills that betrayed the trust of his constituents.

"I was gonna go through this back door over by the men's bathroom," Rooney said while discussing the moment he turned to the dark side. "I was gonna go vote 'no' and I was gonna run. I literally put the card in and there was nobody in the room, and behind me I hear a voice saying 'what are you doing shit head.' It was like literally Darth Vader behind me and I turn around and there is [John] Boehner [former Speaker of the House]. I'm like 'where the hell did you come from?' and he said 'you know the right vote for you is a yes' and I changed my vote." The reporter seemed both humored and horrified.

"You got rolled?" she asked.

"I got rolled," Rooney replied with his head hanging low. Only a man who knows his political career is over is honest.

Changing a vote means you got rolled, but what do you say about someone whose entire character changes to suit a political goal? In the case of Governor George Wallace, he didn't just get rolled; he swan dived into the worst decisions of his life. After his inauguration, Wallace had to turn rhetoric into action, because after all, his audience was waiting for him to deliver the prophecy of Asa Carter.

Something in him felt like this was beyond a job, he felt everything he had to do, he had to hit like an opponent in the ring. During college, Wallace sold magazines door to door and drove a taxi to pay for school, while the other students went to events and enjoyed themselves. After returning from WWII, he hitchhiked from Mobile to Montgomery to personally ask the governor for a job where sooner or later he was appointed to Assistant Attorney General of Alabama. Wallace didn't crawl, barter, and fight just so he could be Governor of Alabama, he always wanted to be something bigger.

On June 11, 1963, Wallace was given his moment in the ring he'd been waiting for. Congress that year passed a bill ruling for the desegregation of all public universities, something which drew immense outrage in Alabama. Days before students at the University of Alabama were able to register for classes, protests had already begun to break out throughout the state, since the school had accepted its first black students. There was an expectation that Wallace would stop it from happening, and while part of him may have felt that this time was when things would start to change for black Americans, the dark side of him knew this was an opportunity to make George Wallace a household name. Civil rights be damned, Wallace was going to put on a show for the whole country.

A friend and former state senator, John Tyson, was on the phone with Wallace as he wondered whether to activate the National Guard to block entry of black students into the school, or go down himself and stand at the doorway. Tyson pleaded with Wallace to accept the new rules and ensure there would be no violence or riots.

"Sometimes in your position as an elected official in command, you have to act on what people are going to do or what they think is right, irregardless of whether it's right or wrong or what have you," Wallace told Tyson. The die was cast, Wallace was driving to Tuscaloosa the next day. Deep down in Tyson's gut, he prayed that Wallace making a spectacle of himself would prevent the National Guard from having to deploy down there to occupy the school if riots were to occur. He couldn't tell whether he feared Wallace making the worst decision possible or trusted him not to make a decision that would negatively impact his political career.

The press arrived at the University including a crowd of hundreds of protestors on both sides of the issue. Anticipating Wallace would do something drastic, President Kennedy, who already formally warned Wallace days prior to not get in the way of the black students, sent down

Deputy Attorney General Nicholas Katzenbach to confront Wallace if he did. Wallace rode up in his motorcade, looking through the tinted windows at the angry, screaming crowds. Seymour Trammell sat beside him, wondering what was going on in the Governor's head as they rode up to the school.

"What do you think?" Wallace asked Trammell.

"I think you need to walk as cocky as a quail and tell them how it's gonna be," Trammell replied. Wallace nodded his head to Trammell as a sign of acknowledgement, and opened his door as soon as the car parked. He stood up as the media rushed over, as well as the crowds of protestors. He fixed his tie, adjusted his jacket, and strutted over to the Registrar's door as if he owned the place. Whether protestors were cheering his name or cursing him, all he cared about was that he was the center of attention.

"I hereby denounce and forbid this illegal and unwarranted action by the central government," Wallace said as he stood in the doorway. Katzenbach walked over and tried to ask Wallace one more time to step away from the door, but instead Wallace took the opportunity while the eyes of the country were on him to discuss how the federal government was crossing the line by deliberately ignoring state's rights. Wallace got what he wanted, the show was about the students who could finally attend college and he took this opportunity to amplify his name recognition. Katzebach received word from President Kennedy after Wallace refused the final warning, that now the National Guard would be federalized, meaning as Governor of Alabama, Wallace had no control over his troops until further notice. General Henry Graham of the Alabama National Guard walked over to Wallace, who stood proud before the crowds and the cameras knowing this whole incident was just about to wrap up.

"Sir, it is my sad duty to ask you to step aside under the orders of the President of the United States," Graham stated to Wallace as he lifted his right hand to salute the Governor. Wallace smiled, returned the salute, shook the General's hand and walked as cocky as a quail back to his car. Once again, Wallace would lose the legal battle, but in the court of public opinion, he was on top of the world.

On September 15, 1963, members of the United Klans of America sect of the KKK blew up the 16th Street Baptist Church in Birmingham, killing four black children and wounding many others. Later that day, two more black children were shot in the street by cops who were responding to a fight between the boys and a group of white kids. In order to quell any violence, Wallace ordered 300 policemen to occupy the streets. Days following the bombing, instead of promoting piece or at least attempting to pretend to appear sympathetic, Wallace told a *New York Times* reporter that there would need to be some more "few first-class funerals" so that the people would give up on the fight for civil rights for good.

As sit-ins at segregated diners were organized by Dr. Martin Luther King and other activists, the world got to witness more brutality inflicted by the police under Wallace's administration, as dogs were unleashed on non-violent activists and many others were blasted with fire hoses. Wallace's response to all of this? Obey the police, respect the law, and don't expect any sympathy from his office if you dared defy either of those instructions. This was Wallace's world, and everyone was just living in it.

In 1964, the polls showed Johnson was weak enough for Wallace to jump in and enter the Democratic primary for the upcoming election. By calling Johnson a big government tyrant who was soft on communists, just as he called Kennedy prior to his assassination in 1963, Wallace began picking up steam in the south and began to worry the Democratic establishment. What began to steal much of Wallace's momentum, however, was Republican candidate Barry Goldwater's shared opposition to the 1964 Civil Rights Act. Goldwater opposed the bill not on grounds of race, but because he felt it was an unconstitutional breach into private property rights by the federal government, which would only make things worse by backing disgruntled whites into a corner. Because of this awkward moment in the election, as both small, but loud groups of conservatives and southern Democrats began to flock to his campaign, Wallace dropped out as not to weaken the Democratic ticket as a whole, knowing as well he wouldn't be able to take on and defeat an incumbent president within his own party. This campaign, however, was less about trying to become president, and more about making a point. This flirtation with the presidency wasn't for nothing though, Wallace enjoyed traveling the country calling protestors "little pinkos" and at times leading the national conversation.

As activists across the country were murdered, beaten, and abused by law enforcement and the KKK, as buses were firebombed as well as people's homes, Wallace looked away from all that and smiled to every camera pointed at him. As governor he felt he had a mandate, and his mandate didn't involve the people who didn't vote for him.

Colin didn't respond to my calls or texts after he quit Corey's campaign. From what mutual friends told me, he was cutting politics out of his life entirely and that meant focusing on the things that ultimately mattered to a kid in college — money, girls, friends and grades. I was upset but I respected his decision. If cutting out all politics meant he had to cut me out to avoid the temptation of getting back in the game, that was what he had to do.

Dwayne on the other hand, months after I gave him what little cash I had and bought back his laptop from the pawn shop, quit the Congressman's office. Rumor was that he also may have been fired —

the story changes depending on who tells it; ultimately, that doesn't matter. One trusted staffer said Dwayne sexually assaulted a female intern, and after he was warned to watch his actions, he did it again to another woman. Another guy I knew who worked for a different representative said he started coming to work hungover, and would regularly drink in the office. I don't know what was truth or fiction, but the reality was somewhere in the mix of accusations. Either way, Dwayne stopped speaking to me after he left D.C. and moved somewhere out near Arlington. Maybe he was trying to cut out politics from his life, thus cutting me out too. The truth was somewhere in the jumbled mess of my confused thoughts as I realized my only friends wanted nothing to do with me.

Sabrina and I drove down to Lynchburg to visit her brother. It was a long ride but something about shedding off the Beltway atmosphere as you saw the neighborhoods go from suburban to rural did something for the soul. Lynchburg was a small town that wanted to be a big city, but still kept that quiet, southern community feel to it. That night, we got dinner with her brother and his girlfriend at a local BBQ joint downtown.

"Where's your family from, Art?" He asked me while I was sucking the meat off a rib. Sabrina luckily jumped in so I didn't have to talk with my mouth full.

"Art's mother is from Alabama but she grew up in Virginia, and his dad is from Cuba but changed his name from Salazar to Brown to sound more American," she said.

"I love Alabama! Where in Alabama is she from?" he asked as soon as I was ready to speak.

"Some town named Clio, but the story changes from time to time; her parents left in the sixties to come to Virginia. I don't know why they don't talk about it but that part of my family was filled with alcoholics or something — something not worth talking about. I think they just wanted a fresh start or whatever when they moved here," I replied.

"You should try one of those ancestry DNA tests to see what pops up; that'd be so interesting, like solving a mystery," the brother's girlfriend said.

"I've tried to get Art to do it but he's never been interested. I'll just have to swab his cheek when he's sleeping and find out myself," she said, getting a laugh out of everyone.

"If I'm related to Castro I'm gonna puke," I said, grabbing another rib off the plate.

The next day while her brother was off working his morning shift in town, Sabrina and I drove to the Shenandoah Valley to see the landscapes from atop the mountains. It had been so long since I did anything for myself other than spending mindless hours on Facebook or researching something politics related. Driving up those long and winding roads, I felt almost guilty. I wasn't working at the time, but I felt like I should have been working or preparing for the next race. But would there be a next race? I'd be lucky after the embarrassment to my career that was Gordan Pecker.

Sabrina and I pulled over to a scenic stop and just stared into the distance. We hadn't spoken much the last week as I went from meeting to meeting trying to secure another client for the 2018 primary season. We talked about many things, our stresses, our hopes, but above all what my next plan was.

"I want to talk to you about the offer from the PAC supporting Ed Gillespie this cycle," I said. After about a week of thinking about it, I finally came to a decision and wanted to tell her first before I spoke to anyone else about it.

"I need to say something first," she jumped in, "I'll support any decision you want to make. I know this is your passion, and I know how hard it is to find someone willing to pay decently for what you do, even though you know I think you deserve so much more." I was taken aback;

that wasn't what I was expecting, but it took some pressure off of me to say what I'd wanted to for the past several days.

"I'm not taking the job" I told her. "He's a piece of shit and there'll be days where I'm rich and days where I'm poor, but I'm not going to bend over for a man with no chin. It's not a hard decision to make; the show goes on, but I get to decide where it goes." She smiled a smile at me more genuine than any I'd seen in a long time. Sabrina was going to stay with me for the long haul; there was no love in politics.

As we walked back to the car, I got a phone call. It was Gordon, who I hadn't heard a peep from in eight months. I was hesitant to pick up the phone at first, but I knew if I didn't he'd keep calling.

"Art, my man, it's so good to get a chance to talk to you again!" He said. I was really hoping he was calling just to chat and nothing more.

"It's good to hear from you too Gordon, what's up?" I asked.

"I'm doing really good. I started going to AA on Wednesdays, and I'm volunteering with my church. My wife and I are legally separated, but she's giving me more opportunities to spend time with my children. I made a lot of mistakes, but I'm trying to be better for it." For a moment I was actually happy for Gordon, but there it was again, that feeling in my gut to get ready for something to happen. "Anyway, I heard you're out of town, but when you get back, I think I might have someone you'd like to work with if you have a chance. Maybe we can meet up for lunch and I'll introduce you two after church this Sunday." I paused for a moment, was this a trap? I thought to myself, this was all just too strange.

"Sure man, let's do it Sunday," I said. I hung up my phone and got into the car with Sabrina. She saw the confused look on my face, knowing something strange had occurred during that brief phone call.

"Who was it?" she asked.

"Either the Devil or a truly reformed Gordon, maybe a strange mix of both but I don't really know at this point," I replied.

The rest of the week we were there visiting her family, I avoided my laptop and talk of politics the entire time, just trying to be in the moment as much as possible, but something just didn't feel right. Gordon was in the back of my mind, but at least for once I didn't feel dragged down by the demons — including the Satan Nixon figure that followed me with every drop of alcohol — that would force me to jump into a tailspin of paranoia and conspiracy, wondering what would happen at that lunch and what other mess Gordon was going to try and pull me into.

Did I do good by Sabrina? I thought so, and for that week she saw I was putting in the effort. However, did the potential thrill of another round of electoral gladiators entice me to at least not cancel my lunch meeting with Gordon and his mystery client? Let's just say I'd sooner be quitting alcohol than politics.

CHAPTER 8

Age of Rage

His fist pounded the podium as flashes from cameras could be heard going off like gunfire. George Wallace was responding to the press regarding the civil rights activists who intended to cross through Selma in 1965 after Wallace made it clear he wouldn't allow it on the grounds he believed a potential riot would ensue. "We won't tolerate a bunch of negro agitators trying to orchestrate a disturbance in this state, not as long as I'm governor." He said, wearing his pressed black suit flanked by Confederate flags draped from each pillar at the Montgomery courthouse. "I stand here today, in the cradle of the confederacy, to remind our people of our founding fathers' goals of duty, goals long since forgotten by progressives and liberals in favor of what they call a 'changing world'."

Darth Vader had stripped himself of any evidence that Anakin Skywalker ever lived. This George Wallace standing before the crowds, warning of a potential riot in Selma, whether he believed his words or not, was now a full-on Sith Lord. Asa Carter's prophecy was now complete; white nationalists had a champion against the civil rights movement. Now Carter, the Emperor to Wallace's Vader, could sit back and watch the whole world burn. There was a riot, but not the one Wallace expected. The riot at the infamous bridge in Selma was a police riot, in which millions across the nation watched as police in riot gear knocked out women and beat men who tried to run away.

Wallace was paranoid, he was already afraid of something going on in Alabama, as rumors circulated that as soon as MLK entered the state, he held a secret meeting with black radical Malcom X. "Is every spook militant in existence gonna pay Alabama a visit?" Wallace said to one of his advisors before the police riot in Selma. By then, the large and looming national issue was the National Voters Rights Act of 1965, which would eliminate poll taxes and literacy tests which prevented many blacks and poor whites in Alabama from voting. Up until this point, Wallace always knew blacks would one day receive the full right to vote, but what he could not tolerate was defiance or disrespect in any form. His ego had fully overtaken his conscious; the dark side was all that remained inside of him as the nation had its eyes on Alabama.

"Are you trying to fuck over your president?" President Lyndon Baines Johnson said to Wallace as they sat across from each other in the Oval Office. Due to overwhelming political pressure to pass the voter's rights bill, Johnson invited his former rival to the White House in an attempt to win him over. While Kennedy was loved by the nation, Johnson was only ever tolerated, a pawn used as nothing but a living, breathing placeholder, nothing more and nothing less up until the 1960 Democrat   convention in order to swing the election to win Texas as well as purple southern states. He easily defeated Goldwater in 1964 more on account of a nation still mourning the loss of John Kennedy, and less about their personal feelings towards Johnson.

Johnson had been a political creature his entire life, much like Wallace. Both born into poverty with an eager eye set on higher aspirations and power. Both FDR style New Deal Democrats, Johnson was more concerned with keeping Democrats in power than anything else, and that meant finding any means necessary in order to take the historic Republican voter bloc in the black community and take it away through expansion of the welfare state which would entice lower income communities, predominantly black communities. None of his actions were done out of care for blacks; Johnson only saw black Americans as pawns, not people.

In discussions with his aides as to whether or not they should continue with supporting the Supreme Court nomination of Thurgood Marshall or appoint another credible black jurist, Johnson turned to them, "When I appoint a nigger to the court, I want everyone to know he's a nigger." Johnson knew that if he wanted the bill to succeed, he needed Wallace to make his police stop hitting people so they had enough time to calm the American people down.

"Well are you trying to fuck me or not? You've seen those protestors outside the window keeping my Lady Bird up at night, why won't you let the niggers vote?" Johnson said, leaning closer to Wallace as an attempt to use his height to intimidate him like a high school bully. This boxing match wasn't going to be a fair fight, Wallace acknowledged, because there was no way playing around with an opponent like Johnson, who was of the same stock as him and was also now the elected leader of the nation, would end well.

"They can already vote in Alabama, Mr. President, but the voting specifics are done by the county registrars who are independent from the executive branch. I have no authority over them," Wallace replied. Johnson, a man known for his wicked temper, was losing patience.

"Governor Wallace, your career has always been about working for the poor, why are you so focused on this black thing?" Johnson asked. What Wallace said next is unknown based off conflicting testimonies, but apparently it just pissed off Johnson even more. "You need to stop thinking less about 1965 and more about 1995 when you're dead and buried. What do you want people to think of you thirty years from now? The man who pushed the country forward, or a racist in the ash heap of American history?" Wallace leaned back, unphased by Johnson's attempt to put him in the corner. The boxer knew going into the Oval Office he wasn't going to knock him out, so he might as well walk out of that room tied.

"I don't right care what they think, and you shouldn't either," Wallace said to Johnson. Wallace wasn't thinking about 1965; instead he was thinking about 1968, and occupying the seat where Johnson sat in the Oval Office.

In 1967, Wallace was constitutionally forbidden from running for a second consecutive term in office, but his White House aspirations required him to have a foothold in Montgomery so he could buck the whole system by launching an independent bid for president. He couldn't have picked a random person or a friend to champion on the campaign trail, only to risk getting stabbed in the back. Wallace devised a plan so drastic, it makes the Netflix series *House of Cards* look lazy. Wallace convinced his team of close advisors that in order to keep control of the Governor's mansion, as well as, have a staging ground for his campaign, he would have his wife Lurleen run.

Lurleen was hesitant; she had recently gone through surgery to stop the spread of a vicious cancer that almost killed her, and their young children still needed their mother. Apart from that, she knew her hollow marriage to George would be dragged through the mud on the campaign trail in Alabama as her opponents would call her a puppet and a tool. God only knows what went through her head as she considered running for governor while her husband planned a race for the White House. Somehow, either because she believed in her husband or because she was too weak or scared to oppose him, she announced her bid for the governor weeks later, and with her husband at her side, became an instant frontrunner.

Lurleen easily won the Democratic primary, but for the first time in Alabama history where the majority black population could vote thanks to the 1965 Voters Rights Act, it looked like her Republican challenger had an actual chance of taking on the wife of the man who cried out "segregation today, segregation tomorrow, segregation forever." Many blacks were skeptical of how Lurleen Wallace would be different than her controversial husband, and for good reason. As the campaign progressed, Lurleen began to address issues that she felt were important to her, developing more of her own voice, and less of as a surrogate for her husband. However, despite George's opposition to civil rights, Wallace as Governor of Alabama built hundreds of trade schools, and gave new and free textbooks to public schools and community colleges, as well as, implementing new job training programs and welfare programs for the blind, mentally ill, and destitute senior citizens. While Americans across the country might have an idea of how blacks in Alabama viewed Wallace, black voters had to ask themselves if their lives were better now than they were four years ago.

For one black woman in Alabama, she knew full well, head clear, that she was going to go to the polls and vote for Lurleen Wallace. Her son, on the other hand, attorney J.L. Chestnut, the same J.L. Chestnut who went and practiced law before Judge George Wallace and defended civil rights activists criminalized by the administration of Governor George Wallace, was dumbfounded.

"Momma," Chestnut said to his mother as the two sat down in her kitchen to drink coffee the day before the 1967 election, "you must be out of your mind. You can't do that to me; I'm one of the leading civil rights lawyers in the south." His mother, a career school teacher, was perfectly sane, that was what bothered him.

"Look," she said after taking a sip of her coffee, "George Wallace has built trade schools all over this state, George Wallace has raised the salaries of teachers three times in a row. That has never happened in my lifetime. And now we have free textbooks in the schools; now look at all that and see the cat running against Wallace. I don't care who my son is, I'm voting for Wallace." Mrs. Chestnut, along with many other blacks who could vote without dealing with a poll tax or a literacy test, a discriminatory practice which George stood and defended, came out to vote for Lurleen the very next day. Lurleen won not just with a major lead over her Republican opponent, but also won a majority of the black vote in the state, a result no one saw coming for a candidate married to the man who would go down in history as the villain of the civil rights movement in America.

Now that the former First Lady was now Governor of Alabama, this gave George the opportunity to control things from the shadows as he went and announced his campaign for the 1968 election for President of the United States soon after she was inaugurated in January of that year. George's right hand man, Seymour Trammell, was responsible for handling the contracts of all major businesses who wanted to set up shop or expand to Alabama on behalf of Governor Lurleen Wallace. Trammell, known amongst friends as George's "hatchet man" and "son of a bitch," made sure that no business could come to Alabama without dropping a significant donation to the coffers of the George C. Wallace presidential campaign.

George was unleashed; now it was time for the nation to get to see him up close and personal as he raged against the machine, coast to coast. After his stunt at the University of Alabama in 1963 and his brief flirtation with the Democratic nomination in 1964, he had started getting accustomed to the national scene and talking to crowds that were quite different than the white southerners in Alabama he spent his entire life molding himself to lead. At an event back in Alabama as his campaign for the White House kicked off, Wallace discussed his appeal to voters in the north, talking about his visit to Milwaukee where he had been invited to speak to an event hosted by an organization that viewed him has a fighter for state's rights. "There were at least a hundred Confederate flags in south Milwaukee and the band played Dixie, and even the Milwaukee Journal had to report this. They played Dixie and 3,500 people stood up and sung it in Polish, and I'll tell ya that Dixie sounds good sung in Polish."

Wallace's campaign promises were simple; reign in the expanding federal government, restore law and order, and pull out of Vietnam within ninety days if the likelihood of victory couldn't be achieved. His stances on domestic and foreign policy made it difficult for professional pundits and pollsters to predict who he'd take more votes away from—the Democrat or the Republican. His mere existence as a credible candidate in the 1968 election was a rebuke of the progressive Democrat establishment and of the neoconservative Republican Party. "The two parties have created a Frankenstein monster, and the chickens have come home to roost all over this country," Wallace said before a crowd of thousands during a campaign trip to California. "There's not one dime of difference between the national Democratic Party and the national Republican Party." Wallace would run a purely populist campaign, funded by the working and middle class voters who loved his message to send what cash they had to spare, and the kickbacks from the contracts secured by Trammell. By also announcing that his beliefs on segregation had changed, he widened his net of appeal to voters in the midwest and east coast. The Wallace war machine was in high gear, and no one in D.C. or the media could predict it'd be as powerful as it was.

On March 31, 1968, President Johnson went before the nation on television and radio to declare he would not be seeking the Democratic nomination for president at that year's convention. While Johnson explained that he wanted to take the high road and stated he was doing so in order to spend as much time as possible working on negotiations in Vietnam in order to end bombings in the north so an opportunity for potential peace could occur, the unpopular truth was that he was incredibly worried he would suffer from another heart attack, much like the one that nearly killed him a decade prior and killed his father when he was around Lyndon's current age at the time. If he did spare the country anything, it was the thought of them wondering if they'd re-elect another president only for him to become incapacitated like Wilson or Franklin Roosevelt, or die in office in the middle of an incredibly unpopular war.

April 4th, Dr. Martin Luther King Jr. was shot and killed by an assassin, plunging the country into a night of sadness and terror that resulted in riots in America's inner cities. In a way, his death seemed almost prophesied by King himself. Months earlier, King told a large congregation that "I might not get there with you, to the promise land." In a year defined by turmoil, especially because of Johnson's escalation of combat forces in Vietnam, many regular people asked how much worse could things really get in a time of so much violence and fear already. All they had to do was wait two months and everything was gonna get so much worse.

Weeks later, tragedy struck the Wallaces personally. For the last several months while her husband was on the campaign trail for his presidential campaign, Lurleen's cancer came back more aggressive than ever. She knew as well as her doctors that this time it was going to kill her. Lurleen's only wish was to die at home surrounded by her children. "If I could just see my children grow up, that's all I want" Lurleen said to her close friend Syble Simon. George took several weeks off from the campaign to come tend to his family in their darkest hour. On April 13th, George walked out of the master bedroom and over to his son George Jr. "Mother isn't going to make it," he said to the boy. Lurleen slipped into a coma which she never woke up from. George brought the children into the room to say their goodbyes. George held her hands as she laid dying and whispered into her ear "Lurleen, the children and I are here, please squeeze my hand if you can hear me." She squeezed his hands, and

George kissed her on her forehead one last time. "Goodbye sweetheart" were the last words he ever said to her.

At Lurleen's funeral, as George and his son were walking back to their car, he shared a tender moment with George Jr. telling him, "You don't understand it now, but as the years go by you'll understand the depth of affection people had for your mother, and that will sustain you." George took two weeks off from the campaign to mourn with his three children before leaving once again to make his case across the nation.

On June 5th, several months after the murder of Dr. King, Democratic frontrunner Robert F. Kennedy was shot and killed at the Ambassador Hotel in California after winning that state's primary just hours before. Wallace, just like every other American citizen, watched on TV as another Kennedy was shot down before our eyes. Politics was a game as George knew better than most, but the threat of violence was real. Kennedy was loved and was expected to win the presidency and restore Camelot and the vision of what his brother couldn't achieve, but none of that was able to stop one man with a gun. Wallace knew he was perhaps the most divisive man in America, he would have to take chances, but not yet.

Coast to coast, city to city, wherever Wallace went, a crowd of supporters were there waiting for him, including the screaming and motivating crowds of protestors yelling "Ooh ahh, Wallace is a pig, ooh ahh, Wallace is a pig." Wallace loved the attention from the protestors because it ensured the media would be there to cover him.

"Just keep on doing what you're doing; you get me a million votes each time you show up," Wallace said, joining in laughter as he continued to make fun of the protestors showing up trying to drown him out from his own rally. "Come up here after my speech and I'll autograph your sandals for ya." The show went on, and at one point in the middle of the general election, as former Vice Presidents Hubert Humphrey and

Richard Nixon received their party's formal nominations, Wallace had a commanding lead of the popular vote.

"On a nationwide basis I would say the daring and the persistence of George Wallace will make him a very formidable third party candidate that might carry several states and maybe 15 percent of the popular vote and may be the deciding factor in the 1968 election," said Tom Wicker of *the New York Times* during a televised broadcast. Daring was an accurate term to describe Wallace's rhetoric, especially after the riots that broke out at the Democratic National Convention in Chicago caused by the leftist organization Students for a Democratic Society.

Hubert Humphrey, the establishment pick who many saw as a continuation of Johnson's administration, was a mere sideshow attraction at his own coronation as fights broke out inside and outside the convention. Inside, delegates who were either on the fence or considering throwing their votes to George McGovern were bribed or beaten by Democratic Party boss and corrupt Chicago Mayor Richard Daley, who even had his goons rough up *CBS* reporter Dan Rather as Rather was attempting to follow a delegate from Georgia who was being dragged out by several of Daley's men. Humphrey and his "politics of joy" as he tried to brand it were lost in the chaos of the convention. The man who Johnson once joked about "having his pecker in my pocket" dropped twenty points in the polls the day after receiving the nomination. As journalist Hunter S. Thompson reported of the 1968 race, "Richard Nixon is the president today because of what happened in Grant Park that night."

Nixon, a former vice president but more recently a two-time loser, thanks to the unpopular Johnson administration and calamity in Chicago, held a solid lead in the polls. Nixon's main task was to not rock the boat at that point, and hope Wallace wouldn't take too many states away thus throwing the election into the House of Representatives, where he felt Humphrey could take the White House from him.

Days after the Chicago riot during a rally in Miami, Wallace spoke to the crowd, telling them, "If the police in this country could just run it for about two years we could go walk in the parks and in the streets safely." Taking an already tense moment in American history isn't unique to Wallace, but he really made people freak out as he warned them of everything from rapists hiding in bushes to anarchists, communists, and hippies burning down white, suburban neighborhoods. "If you get molested on the street, he's out of jail before you get to the hospital and on Monday the police officer is on trial instead of the molester."

Wallace's trip to New York was downplayed by the media when he announced he'd be holding a rally at Madison Square Garden. Instead, Wallace packed the stadium with middle class New Yorkers that felt left out by progressive policies. Like always, the protestors followed and reminded everyone if Wallace hated one thing in the world more than anything else, it was the hippies. "I love you too, I sure do," Wallace said to a long haired, male hippie cursing at him from a set of bleachers, "oh, I thought you were a 'she', you're a 'he' my goodness," he said as the crowd burst out in laughter. Unlike many politicians, Wallace fed off of his haters, and perfected his insults and banter like an art form.

While at a rally in Oregon, towards the end of his speech, Wallace got a bit more hostile than he typically did. He clutched his microphone and stared directly at a bunch of hippies flipping him the middle finger, "I'll tell you what," he said directly to them, "I might not teach you any politics if you listen but I'll teach you some good manners." Wallace was the man in the arena, and he loved every minute of it he could soak up.

While his rhetoric was tough, his stances on certain issues were questionable. The man who once drew a line in the sand on segregation was now trying to paint himself as less of a racist and more of a state's rights supporter. His most contentious interview of that cycle was on *Firing Line*, hosted by *National Review* founder and editor William F. Buckley Jr. Buckley tried to call out Wallace for backtracking on his support of segregation and more as the men cut each other off and spoke over each other the entire time, and at certain points even ganging up on the moderator between the two of them.

"We don't have segregation in Alabama," Wallace said, "We've had more mixing and mingling of people of both races in Alabama than you've had in New York state where you come from." He tried to add, as well, that he never supported federal segregation and wouldn't as president. In Buckley's attempt to discredit Wallace's conservative supporters that were made up of disenfranchised middle and working class Republicans, he tried to reference an article of *Human Events* in which 200 "prominent conservatives" disavowed Wallace as a conservative candidate. Buckley's apparent dislike for Wallace made it easy for Wallace to knock his argument down.

"200 prominent conservatives, that's typical of what you'll hear from people who write in magazines," he said to Buckley. "Who are these prominent conservatives? I can go out here and no one will know," he said gesturing to the audience. "I don't know any prominent conservative, and in the first place we've overestimated the power of what the editor of a magazine can do." The only moment of levity came when Wallace spoke of why he hated *Time Magazine*, specifically because of an article written where the reporter said Wallace made a sucking sound with his teeth and picked his teeth with a dirty toothpick. Neither men truly won the spat on national TV, but Wallace came out of it rather clean, while Buckley may have accidentally drawn Wallace more conservative support from those who viewed Buckley trying to throw as many hits as possible, none of them leaving any marks on Wallace, however.

Buckley would point out what historical scholars would question for decades to come, whether or not Wallace really had any ideals he really cared about or if he'd say and do anything to stay politically relevant. There is a story where at one rally, a reporter from *the New York Times* brought his son to work with him while covering a Wallace rally. Wallace, who complained the media wasn't televising the full extent of the crowds in attendance, put all the press in attendance in a caged off section in the middle of the rally close to the podium, so he could chastise them and call them names like "communists" and "liars." The boy grew scared as Wallace pointed out his father, saying he worked for the "Moscow Times" as the crowds of Wallace supporters screamed at the press, calling them traitors and enemies of the country.

At the end of the day, the reporter and his son retired to the hotel room they had, which happened to be at the same hotel as the rest of the press in attendance, including Wallace and his campaign team. As the two began to relax, they heard a knock on the door. The reporter went over and opened it, shocked as he realized it was Wallace's press secretary.

"Governor Wallace would like to speak to you and your son in his room," the secretary said. They went over to Wallace's suite, and as they walked in saw Wallace sitting in a chair. Wallace called the boy over, picked him up and sat him on his lap like a grandfather would his grandchild.

"Son, you know those things I said about your daddy?" he said to the boy, "don't pay them no attention and never mind them, that's just politics." In a moment like that you have to really wonder, was Wallace saying that because he felt sorry for the kid whom he scared? Or was it to cleanse a guilty conscience? What other things had Wallace said that were just politics?

On Election Day, Wallace carried five states, Humphrey carried thirteen plus D.C., and Nixon won with thirty-two. Wallace was defeated, but he felt far from being a loser. While Nixon was able to channel the turnout of the silent majority, Wallace made it known to the country that the ten million voters who showed up for him were out there, and that his reach was far beyond the southern states he carried.

CHAPTER 9

Mr. Nobody...

I met Gordon at a coffee shop in his neck of the woods, a few hours drive from my place in the beltway and far enough to no longer see a plane aiming at Ronald Reagan or Dulles airports. He shaved, even wore a nice Mr. Rogers-esue sweater that made him seem like the guy you'd run into at a church potluck. It was strange seeing Gordon this way, sober. To his right was an older gentleman named Skip Miller, a former high school teacher who now operated his own real estate business. The real estate market on this side of the Potomac wasn't anything to brag about, but Skip was happy keeping himself busy after retirement.

Gordon convinced Skip to run for city council this upcoming election, for a seat that hadn't been held by a Republican since Nixon was president. Gordon knew if he wanted to get back into the good graces of the local Republican social circles, he had to earn it, and by managing a campaign, he knew he could force people to accept him whether they wanted to or not. Skip had run for office previously in the nineties, running against the incumbent mayor of over thirty years, Alister Short,

Jackson Short's father. Miller seemed like a nice man, but apparently there was bad blood between him and Short.

"It's been decades since that election so most locals won't even remember it ever happened. Besides, I'm friends with Jackson, and I doubt Alister is still holding a grudge after all that time," Jackson said. "Art, I need you to work the ground game while I work as Skip's face for the right connections and the press. I know we'll be able to take this seat easily, and you'll get a good paycheck out of it, too." I felt uncomfortable. I didn't want to say it, but it hadn't been a full year since Gordon just flamed out in front of the entire county. I wouldn't have even bought a car from him if I knew who he was. Still, I'd be working for Mr. Miller, not Gordon, and I needed the money, so beggars can't be choosers.

I was staying at a cheap hotel at night and working from Miller's basement and from my car during the day, making phone calls, working with the three or four volunteers we had, and soliciting donors. It was an all-day gig, but Miller was good to me, and he treated me better than any other candidate I ever worked for. This campaign felt nice, refreshing, we focused on real issues like revitalizing tourism, lowering taxes, and helping our schools. Everything was going fine, but quickly I began to realize I hadn't heard from Gordon in a while. It was as if he vanished from the face of the earth.

"Art," I heard Skip call from his living room, "you better head over here." He had the TV turned onto the local news. Another candidate named Alexander Donner, a younger black man with a truly magnetic Obama-like charm that ate up the camera, was announcing his bid for mayor- as a Republican. That wasn't the concern, the concern was that Gordon was on screen standing right beside him. "That son of a bitch, he turned on us!" Skip yelled out.

There was literally one week until the Republican endorsement committee meeting, where several hundred dues paying Republicans would turn up to endorse a candidate for the election. It made no sense that Donner would jump in the race without serious backing, and it made less sense to see Gordon, the man who recruited Skip to run, on television with him. I called Gordon immediately over and over but didn't get as much as the voicemail; he was purposefully rejecting my calls. This was all-out war.

I went back to my hotel close to midnight, finishing a large pepperoni Little Caesars Pizza. I felt like shit, so I ate shit to make myself feel less like shit. With Donner in the race, Republicans ate up the idea of nominating a young black man. Donner had less roots in the city, was a virtual unknown, all the things Skip wasn't, but many local Republican bigwigs were willing to support him because of the "optics." I heard a ringing from my bed. It was Ned, one of our volunteers and two time city council candidate. Gordon brought Ned onto the team as a "specialist" though I didn't know what his specialty was, other than losing. During Ned's last race, he didn't attend a single public event or forum. His excuse was not showing up would make voters "more interested" in the mystery candidate. If he had a specialty, maybe it was licking lead paint as a child.

"Art, how we during on ballot signatures?" he asked me. We needed two hundred registered voters in the city to sign Skip's petition so he could appear on the May ballot, and thanks to Gordon's stunt we were short fifty.

"We're doing fine, we just have another hard day to push so we make sure we have more than the two hundred we need in case some signatures aren't valid, but we should be approved before the committee meeting at the end of the week," I said to him while contemplating ordering another pizza to satisfy my feelings of inadequacy, not wanting to let Skip down but not wanting to lose another race because we couldn't get past a primary challenger from who came in from the shadows.

"Well you know how Skip ran for Mayor way back when? How about we try and find his old ballots and just copy those signatures over to the current petition, there's sure to be some of those folks who still live here, right?" Ned asked. I felt like I walked into the freaking Twilight Zone, a grown-ass man who ran for office twice before — as a virtue signaling Republican no less — recommended committing fraud to save us a day of work. I didn't think too hard before I said what I said next.

"Ned, you're fired and don't you ever fucking call me or Skip again," I said, hanging up the phone. I may not have been nice but it sure as Hell felt good to say that to him, even if he wasn't the person I wanted to really yell at. I reached under my bed and pulled out a bottle of bourbon. I had gone several months without a drop of alcohol. I turned on some music on my laptop, the *Blue* album by the Black Keys, took a swig from the bottle, and tried to fall asleep. For a moment, I felt at peace with the universe, but the universe has a way of taking it away as fast as it was given. I felt a warm hand walking its fingers across my chest, almost like it was teasing me.

"Mr. Big here is finally a campaign manager for a good guy, does it make up for all the other men you helped before who didn't deserve it?" The voice asked. The way it talked looked sounded like Satan Nixon, but this was different, this voice was female. I turned over and saw a skeletal figure of a woman in a pink dress, spattered with blood. It was a monstrous insult of Jackie Kennedy. "You're only sticking by the old man cause you think he'll take you with him to city council! You just don't know when to quit!" She screamed. Before I knew it, I flung myself off the bed and fell onto the cold floor. I tried to catch my breath as my heart raced in my chest. Suddenly, there was a knocking at my door. No one should have been there, it was one o'clock in the morning.

"Who the fuck is it! Who's out there?" I yelled at the door.

"Art, its Ness," the faint voice said. "Please Art, I'm here alone." Was this some type of twisted joke set up by Jackson or Gordon? Was it another sick set up by Satan Nixon or whatever other monster my mind would conjure up to torture me? I couldn't just ignore it, I needed to know who was on the other side of that door so I could get this over with for good and finally catch some sleep.

I walked over to the door and opened it. Vanessa was there, wearing her pajamas under a trench coat, drenched from standing in the rain from earlier in the night. Something was wrong though, she had a black eye and a busted, cut lip. Her eyes were red from crying and her voice was strained. Anger began to grow inside of me at the thought of someone harming her.

"Who did this to you?" I asked, passing her a cup of coffee I made in the room's cheap coffee maker. Vanessa told me how Jackson's father, the Mayor, heard Gordon convinced Skip to run. The Mayor still had it out for Skip from their race three decades ago, so Jackson called Gordon and said if he ever wanted a future in city politics, he'd have to manage the campaign for his chosen candidate, Alexander Donner, so he could keep an eye on him. This way, the Mayor not only got his preferred guy in office, but got his kicks out of seeing Skip lose again while making a pet out of Gordon. I felt like puking; these people were manipulating the course of the local election like it was a sick game. There were real issues affecting real people, but Jackson and his father were too busy playing political kingpins to satisfy an old grudge.

"Jackson also knows if you and Skip win, that'll diminish his family's influence around the county and the state," She said. When Vanessa found out what Jackson and his father were doing, she packed up her things and planned to leave him, but Jackson didn't approve of the breakup. "I called him a pussy and he punched me. I fell down the stairs, but he didn't even come down to do anything else. He just watched me fall and threw my bag down before walking away."

"Why didn't you go to the cops?" I asked her.

"Jackson and his father own the cops, and they funded the sheriff's race. There is no way I'm going to them; no one would believe me," she said, wiping away more tears. Rage coursed through my veins, I wanted to hurt someone so badly.

"I'm gonna call Sabrina. She'll come get you in the morning and you can stay with her for a while." I know what you're thinking, I let her spend the night and something happened, but it didn't. I let her sleep in the bed while I laid out a blanket across the floor, even contemplating getting my bottle of bourbon and sleeping in the tub like old times. The thought of laying down with her once again did cross my mind, like it would any man's in this situation. She was so vulnerable and in need of someone to care for her. I loved her, part of me always had and always would, but much like Colin who cut me out of his life to avoid a path of bad decisions, having Vanessa still involved in mine only made me realize my own mistakes.

Sabrina drove by first thing in the morning to pick up Vanessa. As they loaded up her car with Vanessa's things, I came downstairs to the parking lot, dressed with my white button down shirt, black blazer, and red tie, with the added flair of my Georgetown sweatpants.

"So is this whole outfit on purpose?" Sabrina pointed at me as her eyes checked me out head to toe.

"I need to be in as good a mood as possible, and that means the sweatpants are on until I have to change into something meant for adults," I replied. She giggled at me and I could see Vanessa trying to contain her laughter through the car windshield.

"The moment things get ridiculous, you need to leave You don't owe anyone anything, and you need to take care of yourself, or these people will drag you down and destroy you," Sabrina said, caressing my face with her hand ever so smoothly. I looked over to Vanessa, sitting in the car still with her busted lip and black eye.

"Things are past ridiculous, now I'm out for blood."

Everyone who was everyone in Republican politics was going to drive all the way down to Liberty University for the Republican Senate debate. Corey Stewart, who was going around the state saying Republicans who didn't support him had limp dick syndrome or something like that, was the supposed frontrunner. Delegate Nick Freitas was a favorite amongst young Republicans and was catching up to Corey in the polls. Reverend E.W. Jackson was there running too, but no one really knew why.

Corey had one hell of a last couple months, first having been linked to the Charlottesville riot due to the disturbing number of staffers who were there, then a video was released of him singing the praises of Paul Nehlen, who came out to support Corey all the way from Wisconsin way after he already was outed as a white supremacist during the previous race. Moderate, beltway Corey was all about calling people Yankees with erectile dysfunction in bed with communists and Antifa terrorists. Yet for some dumbass reason, Virginia Republicans were still showing up for a man even President Trump didn't want to go anywhere near. In a way, this was incredibly disappointing, because this wasn't the Corey many people in my neck of the woods remembered growing up. This was a Corey who wanted to win, enough said.

At the end of the debate, the topic of immigration came up and one of the moderators asked a question regarding Stewart's racially tinted rhetoric and whether it was actually helping Republicans statewide or not. Freitas took this opportunity to shed light on the new Corey we'd been witnessing for over a year now.

"My daughter came over to me one day and asked, 'Daddy, what is wrong with our last name?' And it's because two of [Stewart's] field directors were putting out memes that were saying things like 'Freitas sounds like something more on the dollar menu at Taco Bell than it does a U.S. Senate candidate.'" This was the part the audience had been waiting for all night. "I fought for my country. I am every bit as much a citizen as you are, Corey Stewart, and I don't appreciate it when my kids have to ask me that question in this country."

Now, Corey could have denied it, he even could have apologized for it, instead Corey showed just what he was willing to stand by in order to seem as tough as possible. Corey laughed at Freitas for a moment until the moderators gave him a minute to respond. "I pledged to run a vicious and ruthless race against Tim Kaine in November. You know why? Because he's going to run one against us. And if all it takes is to make a little bit of fun of your name by some supporters out there of mine, if that's all it takes to get under your skin, you've got some major problems if you were ever going to get this nomination. I don't think you're gonna do it, but if you did, he's going to eat you up, and spit you out." Corey may have been laughing at Freitas, but the audience was seriously pissed. Much like George Wallace and many before him, Corey gave into the dark side and finally showed who he was unequivocally willing to work with, say, and do whatever it took to win.

I walked out and tried to see if there was anyone I recognized who I could speak to and try to get some support from so I could come home with some good news for Skip. Surprisingly Jackson didn't show up, but Judas in the flesh was there, chatting things up with Corey Stewart himself. I must have been standing in the same place long enough because Gordon looked over and physically looked uncomfortable, as if he saw something unpleasant as he saw me. There was nowhere else to run for him; he was going to have to come over and pay the piper.

"Art, buddy," he said walking over to me. I didn't know whether to say hello back or throat punch him. "I know things look bad right now but you're a professional, I'm a professional..."

"No you're not, Gordon. You're a piece of shit, and you've always been a piece of shit," I said. He stood there, silently; I could tell there must have been a million thoughts going through his head. "I can't tell if you're getting some type of sick pleasure out of doing the shit you do or if you're really as pathetic and weak as everyone thinks you are. You have no redeeming qualities as a human being." His face grew pale, I must have said something that actually hurt him. "I'm going to destroy you at that committee next week, and after this election is over I'm going to make sure when your children hear your name they think of how much of a coward their father is." He looked at me, still not saying anything, then I walked away. What was there to say? I couldn't trust him in this game, and I knew sure well I couldn't trust him period.

I did hear a familiar laugh coming from the corner of the room, a laugh I hadn't heard in more than a year now. I turned around and saw Gordon's new candidate Donner laughing with my good friend Dwayne. I smiled, it was good to see someone who I genuinely liked for a change. I walked over and called out his name, but he didn't turn my way. I got right next to him and Donner, slapping Dwayne on the back.

"Brother! It's great to see you man!" I said while smiling ear to ear, but Dwayne looked uncomfortable, while Donner looked confused as to why I walked over in the first place.

"Uh, sir, I'm sorry but I think you've confused me with someone else," he said. I thought this was a joke or something.

"Funny man, seriously how you been?" Dwayne looked at Donner, who was staring at him, then he looked back at me.

"Sir, I'm sorry but we don't know each other," he said to me. I was stunned, either this was a joke, or he was giving me an ice cold shoulder. Of all the people in the world who'd do this to me, I didn't think for a moment it'd be Dwayne. It stung like very few things could affect me emotionally.

"Dwayne, let's say we go grab Gordon and get some dinner?" Donner said. It all made sense, Dwayne was working for Gordon and Donner, meaning he didn't even want them to know we were friends. It was like getting stabbed right through the heart, now my only other friend didn't even want to acknowledge my existence.

I walked out to my car, ignoring everyone around me as I tried to contain the flurry of emotions and thoughts running through my head. Sitting on the hood of my car was a short brunette with secretarial looking glasses. If she wasn't sitting on the hood of my car I'd probably given her a second look walking by, she was kinda cute, but suddenly a sinking feeling in my gut came out of nowhere warning me something was about to go down.

"Hello, Mr. Brown," she said smiling as she got up and walked towards me. "It's been a while, hasn't it?" she asked. It was Courtney Cole, the woman who beat the shit out of Gordon in the race for city treasurer on the other end of the state, here possibly to kill me for fanning the flames of that rumor that she'd bankrupt the city if elected (in reality she was really good at crunching the numbers and keeping the books orderly. I'm kinda glad she won). This was it, I was gonna get shot in the parking lot. She reached into her purse as she walked towards me and time turned into slow motion as I imagined her pulling out a gun and shooting me in the forehead as my imaginary John McAfee did way back when.

"Wait!" I yelled as I put my hand out, halting her, "I have two things to say." She looked confused. I continued to panic and rabble on. "I was just trying to win the race and be good for my client, who turned out to be a massive dick. That and I ended up voting for you and your hair's real nice and if you shoot me now it'll be hard to cover up for your next election. Well, technically that was four things, but you get my point." She slowly pulled her hand out of her purse, holding a checkbook.

"I'm not here to kill you, Mr. Brown," she said. "I'm here to help you. For one, I heard about what happened on Gordon's campaign; you left when you realized the type of person he was. A real cold-hearted political operative would have stuck it out, but you didn't. Secondly,

Vanessa called me this morning and told me what Jackson did. I'm not a perfect human being, but I won't sit by and let someone go around beating women and getting away with it because of who he is or who his daddy is." She got within an inch of my face and put the check in my suit's breast pocket. "Now you need to go be a good boy and win Skip's race, and let me worry about taking care of Jackson and Gordon." Out of nowhere she grabbed me by the tie and pulled me in for a kiss. Not going to lie, this short woman scared me, but I did enjoy it. I didn't know whether to be turned on or terrified.

"I'll ah...I'll see what I can do," I said as she walked away with that confident smile of hers. I pulled out the check, and as I looked at all the zeros. I immediately knew I needed a Swiss bank account or someone really good with cooking the books. I looked at the memo line which she filled out, "fuck you money." This woman was the most ballsy politician I'd ever met.

George Wallace wasn't a one-off election anomaly, he was a rock band taking a break before the next nationwide tour and everyone felt it in the air during the lead up to the 1972 election, like the calm before the storm. He knew, like everyone else who worked for him, that as a third party candidate for the highest office in the land, he had achieved too much in 1968 just to let it fade into the footnotes of history.

It wasn't just his massive success in 1968 that gave him the motivation to contemplate another run for the White House; it was his new partner in crime, his new wife, Cornelia who pushed him to, as some would say, try and become a better candidate, and perhaps even a better husband, father, and human being.

Cornelia Folsom was a slim, bosomy, long legged, dark haired beauty who was used to turning heads her entire life. In high school she had placed second for Ms. Alabama, but apart from her beauty queen fame, her family connections put her in the circles of the affluent and politically connected. Her mother, "Big Ruby" Folsom, was former Governor Jim Folsom's sister. She first met George a decade before they married, when he was just Jim Folsom's pupil in politics and the "fighting little judge," as local papers called him. Cornelia didn't find him attractive in the slightest, with her friends noting that his resting scowl and short height made him appear like a bulldog, not the type of man a woman of her beauty would be attracted too.

Years went on since their first introduction, however, and both individuals grew personality wise during that time, both bearing the scars of life. After graduating college, Cornelia used her talents as a singer and guitarist to try and make a name for herself in country music, even going on tour in Australia as a guitarist for country singer Roy Acuff. She had her fun and moved back to the States, moving to Florida and getting married, giving birth to two sons, then getting divorced in 1968. She moved back home with Ruby, who threw lavish parties to try and get her daughter a new husband either involved in politics or business, anything to keep her in the life she had grown accustomed to growing up.

When she met George once again, several years after his run for president and long after Lurleen had died, she noticed something different in him. He had what she described as a "feisty walk," a pep in his step that commanded respect and attention from those around him. She liked his style, maturity, and confidence. As for George, he had always had a weakness for beautiful women. The two were smitten by each other, and everyone around them saw them as the new Alabama power couple. The only one to object to their courtship was Big Ruby. Drinking bourbon from an oversized iced tea glass, Ruby sat Cornelia down one afternoon and told her, "Why, honey, he ain't titty high." Shortness aside, Cornelia fell in love with the confident former governor, and he fell in love with her as she brought new energy into his life.

They got married in 1971, just in time for their first political battle. George knew in order to fight once again for the White House from a position of strength, he'd need to take back the Governor's Mansion from the incumbent Governor Albert Brewer. Brewer was Lurleen's Lt. Governor when she died, taking over as Governor of Alabama becoming the first incumbent to run for a consecutive re-election in almost a century thanks to a change in the Alabama constitution that allowed incumbents to run for re-election. This was a tough fight for George, especially since Brewer was both popular among whites and extremely popular among blacks throughout the state and was almost as much of a charismatic leader as George.

Brewer, however, had some backup from an unexpected ally- Republican President Richard Nixon. Nixon understood that if Wallace ran again for president, he would potentially damage him enough to lose his office. During the 1968 campaign, Nixon had to take much of Wallace's talking points and style in order to keep southern Republicans from peeling off. The threat of Wallace was real, so Nixon had his staff make a series of large donations to Brewer's campaign in hopes that by keeping Wallace out of the Governor's mansion, Nixon's re-election would be a landslide.

Governor Brewer took advantage of Wallace's active presidential campaign, calling him out for traveling the country running for president while the state of Alabama needed him to come home and listen to the people and the issues that were important to them, not just battleground states like Iowa. Thanks to Nixon, who secretly funneled a series of large cash donations to Brewer's campaign, the Nixon camp provided him with one third of his donations. Bob Ingram, Brewer's press secretary said it was the cleanest political donation he ever saw. They didn't want a job or a special favor, all Nixon wanted was for Brewer to beat Wallace.

"His presidential ambitions keep him far away from the troubles of Alabama. We need a governor who puts Alabama before himself," Brewer told a crowd of supporters at a rally.

Wallace, a much more grizzled political warrior than Brewer, knew how to drag him into the ring so he could throw as many haymakers as possible to knock him out. Wallace gave Brewer a name that would make Trump's "Lyin' Ted" and "Crying Jeb Bush" look like child's play. Wallace went from city to city calling Brewer "Sissy Britches" instead of by his name, and the crowd ate it up.

There was one thorn in his side during the race other than Brewer however, because there was one candidate running who reminded Wallace of how he became the man he was. Asa Carter, upset that his role in the 1963 race as well as the 1967 race for Lurleen had been diminished from an essential one to a tertiary consultant amongst Alabama's political class after the fact, as well as being left out of the 1968 presidential race entirely, had thrown his KKK hood into the race. Carter decided he had enough of George Wallace and launched an independent campaign for governor based on a white supremacist platform.

Carter travelled the state calling Wallace a race traitor and a liberal for turning his back on segregation, attempting to take away as many disgruntled white votes away from Wallace as possible. Carter's campaign gained very little traction, however. There would continue to be severe racial issues in Alabama for decades to come, but the era of Asa's dream of segregation forever was well behind the people of the state as they moved forward, leaving him behind.

Wallace's re-election, despite his name calling of Brewer and annoyance of Asa Carter, was more like what Wallace had always wanted it to be, more positive and policy focused. It was 1971, and segregation was no longer a topic. Blacks could vote and they gave George as much of a majority as they had Lurleen in 1968. This time, he could focus on jobs, schools, and infrastructure, advocating for the poor like he had always wanted to. Old habits die hard, however, and when the race was reaching the finish line and Wallace found himself neck and neck with Brewer in the polls, Wallace got desperate. Desperation makes a man do desperate things, and while much had changed in Wallace's life, he still had that devil on his shoulder telling him that losers don't legislate. Wallace showed those around him that he may have appeared less volatile on the outside, but on the inside he was still willing to win by any means necessary.

"We gotta do what we gotta do," Wallace said to his staff. What Wallace was referring to 1963, when they pulled out the race card and did whatever was necessary to win. He probably would have been able to win without playing dirty, but he did it anyway. The Wallace campaign published and dispersed hundreds of smear sheets accusing Brewer of being a homosexual, his wife of being an alcoholic, and their daughter of getting knocked up by a black man. Things even got more ridiculous as they forged photos of Brewer standing next to known black militants and communists, accusing him of being a traitor. "There's no reason to let any one group call all the shots in this state," Wallace said to a crowd during one of his last rallies, "and you know if the militant black bloc voting in this state takes over, it's going to control politics over the next fifty years in Alabama, and I know you're not going to let that happen." Maybe in his heart Wallace wanted to run the race like Brewer, but there was that voice in his head that told him if he wanted to win, he'd have to act like Asa Carter.

Wallace beat Brewer narrowly in the Democratic primary and went on to an easy victory in the general election, setting the stage for his 1972 presidential run. Carter's independent bid came in with less than one percent of the total vote in the general election. At Wallace's inauguration, Carter's supporters showed up with signs saying "Wallace is a bigot" and "free our white children!" The inauguration protest was the last time Asa Carter was seen publicly ever again. In 1979, Carter got into a fistfight with his son and died from a fatal heart attack. Wallace's days of being for segregation may have been behind him, but he still spilled blood in the water by using the race as a factor.

Wallace was walking tall after retaking his home in the Governor's mansion, where he first came to political prominence and where his previous wife had died. In an odd way, Wallace had Nixon to thank for the constant media attention thrown at the Alabama race, since by fueling Brewer's war chest he made the race all the more entertaining for the nation to watch, thus creating a stronger enemy in the process.

This proxy war between Wallace and the political elite in D.C. and Alabama allowed him and Cornelia to strengthen their bond as husband and wife, as well as, a political team. As for his personal life, Cornelia made him a happier man, happier than close friends had seen him in years. For Christmas, she even convinced George to dress up as Santa Claus for the kids, embracing her role as a step-mother to his children with full embrace. For the children, their family developed a closeness and bond thanks to Cornelia that they hadn't felt in years.

Cornelia's most obvious change in George's life was his wardrobe. She hated that all he ever wore were the same black suits and black dress shoes like every other politician. A natural born fashionista, Cornelia threw more color into his wardrobe, most famously a broad collared white suit and brown, leather wingtip shoes that oozed style and taste, just as she wanted. She even went as far as to change his hair from that greasy, slicked back style he had used for years, and gave it a much thicker, stylized look that made him appear much younger and hipper. This was George Wallace 2.0, a man with a fresh take on life that most Alabamans, and the country as a whole, hadn't seen of him before.

When Wallace entered the Democratic primary in 1972, he was one of the last candidates to enter the race but immediately was one of the top contenders for the nomination. Choosing to run as a Democrat wasn't his first choice though, which is why he entered the primary race so late in the game. Thanks to his independent campaign in 1968, he sparked the creation of the American Independent Party, a third party which was recognized with major party status in many states thanks to Wallace's work to achieve ballot access in all fifty states that year, which no professional pundit or politician thought he could achieve. The American Independent Party would eventually eat up other smaller third parties at the state level, primarily on the west coast, and in the 1990s would transform into the modern day Constitution Party, a smaller third party than the Libertarian Party, but still able to obtain ballot access in many states every presidential election year.

After attending an American Independent Party convention in the northeast as a speaker, Cornelia was bothered by the appearance and manner of those in attendance at the convention. The attendees were predominantly working class, white men, still bent on discussing racial politics and the threat of the Trilateral Commission and Jewish banking conspiracies. She had recently watched her husband fight tooth and nail for the Governor's mansion, and knew that this third party bid wouldn't just embarrass him going forward, but also was not a true representation as to who he was anymore as a person.

"Is this all you're worth George Wallace? Running for president under the banner of a fringe third party?" she asked on the car ride to the airport. George knew Cornelia was right, so the decision to go forward was obvious. He'd have the support of enough independent conservatives and southern Democrats to potentially win the Democratic nomination, and the White House.

The race for the nomination wasn't easy for Wallace, but every other political battle in his life was a fight. A progressive senator from

South Dakota, George McGovern, was highly favored by young Democrats and the anti-war movement, but he scrapped for delegates to the convention. Former Vice President Hubert Humphrey was running again as the establishment's favorite son, but his failure in 1968 still loomed large. Former Governor and Senator from Maine, Ed Muskie, was an early favorite in the race, but personal issues among him and campaign staff sabotaged him way before the convention. A letter written by Muskie was leaked to the press with derogatory language aimed at Canadians, and after the Iowa Caucus, journalist Hunter S. Thompson of *Rolling Stone Magazine* spread a rumor that Muskie was enlisting the help of a witch doctor from South America to continually craft crazy drugs and potions meant to calm his nerves. The rumor wasn't true, but it was enough to break his will to continue to the convention.

With Senator Ted Kennedy refusing to run in the race, the primary battle between Wallace, McGovern, and Humphrey would get tense, especially as the days to the convention were narrowing down and Democrats had to decide who was ultimately the best candidate to beat Richard Nixon and end the war in Vietnam; would it be former segregationist and third party spoiler George Wallace? A big time loser who lost control of his own convention and the election four years ago Hubert Humphrey? Or the optimistic newcomer with very little baggage, George McGovern? The primaries were still contentious, but the answer grew more apparent every day.

The Wallace factor in this race made it all the more difficult for the other candidates to get any media attention, as Wallace seemed to suck the air out of every room with the press. Much like in 1968, Wallace supporters came out in droves for the boxer from Alabama, and this time they felt that with the Democratic nomination, they'd actually take the White House, thus bucking the Republican Party and Democratic Party establishments. For the most part of the '72 race, Wallace and Cornelia seemed to have more fun on the campaign trail than any of the other candidates. There was a joke amongst non-Wallace supporting Democrats that they'd gladly vote for Cornelia, but wouldn't vote for George.

Cornelia was as much a star as George was at his own rallies. Tom Turnipseed, one of Wallace's primary aides who had also previously worked on his 1968 campaign, said he wanted to capture positive media attention by turning Cornelia into the "Jackie Kennedy of rednecks." Word got back to George of what Tom had said, and George took offense to it, but Cornelia laughed at the concept, even embracing it.

Hot on the campaign trail, Hunter S. Thompson, who chronicled the 1972 election in his reports for Rolling Stone which were compiled into his book *Fear and Loathing on the Campaign Trail '72*, spoke candidly of his feelings of Wallace, as he did everybody. "One of the worst charlatans in politics," he wrote. Thompson was able to understand what many journalists at the time ignored about Wallace, his ability to talk directly to Americans who felt left out of today's political discussion. "Maybe the whole secret of turning a crowd on is getting turned on yourself by the crowd. The only candidate running for the presidency today who seems to understand this is George Wallace ... able to connect with people on some kind of visceral instinctive level that is probably both above and below 'rational politics.'"

Thompson even went on to describe Wallace rallies as being akin to a Janis Joplin concert "in which the bastard had somehow levitated himself and was hovering over us." His reporting was vulgar like all his work, but just as amusing as it was accurate. While reporting from Wisconsin, Thompson reported that "anybody who doubts the Wallace appeal should go out and catch his act sometimes. He jerked this crowd in Serb Hall [American Serb Memorial Hall] around like he had them all on wires. They were laughing, shouting, whacking each other on the back ... it was a flat-out fire and brimstone performance." Wallace may not have been the frontrunner after losing more primaries to McGovern towards the end of the season, but he was given the rockstar treatment like no other candidate.

On May 15th, 1972, on the eve of the Maryland primary, Wallace got out of bed, despite Cornelia's protest to take a day off, to go to final rally. "What good will one more rally do George? You have to rest," she told him. Still, George wanted to knock it out so the two got dressed and walked down the hotel stairs to the limousine waiting to take them to Laurel, Maryland. On that day, another man from out of state would attend the same rally, but for a very different reason.

Arthur Bremer was a social recluse from Milwaukee, Wisconsin. Much like many other stalkers and serial killers, Bremer felt his existence was meaningless, and if he were to earn any type of love and affection, he would need to do something drastic and irreversible. His plan to win the adoration of the world that rejected him was simple- kill either Richard Nixon or George Wallace. Without killing one or both men, Bremer filled living out the rest of his days ignored, forgotten, a true nobody.

The crowd at the Laurel shopping center wasn't anything to brag about but was large enough to still need a good number of security personnel. After Wallace gave his speech, Bremer walked up to a police officer tasked to guard Wallace and asked if George would come down and shake his hand. Wallace didn't plan on staying afterwards to socialize, but thought mingling with his supporters wouldn't be an issue. His lead guard asked for him to stay where he spoke so people could come up to him, this way they could have full visibility and easy control of the crowd should anyone get rowdy.

"It's alright, I'll take full responsibility," George said to the guard. After a few minutes of walking among the crowd and shaking hands, Bremer pushed his way to the front of the crowd where Wallace stood, pulled out a pistol and shot Wallace in the abdomen five times, with the other bullets hitting several guards. Wallace fell to the ground immediately. The guards nearby tackled Bremer, knocking the gun out of his hands as the crowd panicked and dispersed. Cornelia, who was only feet away from George, rushed over to him, laying across his body to protect him from another potential shooter. "I'm...I'm bleeding," George mumbled to her as he quickly lost consciousness.

"George, I'm gonna take you home," she screamed while more cops and paramedics ran over. "I'm gonna take you home, I'm gonna take you home now," she kept repeating to him. Still in shock, the paramedics had to pull Cornelia off of George to get him onto the stretcher. "Don't take me away from my husband!" She yelled again before coming to her senses and letting them rush George to the ER.

I unleashed a plague of biblical proportions upon Alexander Donner's campaign the last four days before the committee meeting. We burned more cash getting ready for that meeting than we would our entire general campaign. We flooded every Republican in the city with enough mailers and flyers to line a hundred bird cages. I even paid ice cream vendors to place our campaign bumper stickers all over their trucks.

Courtney kept her side of the bargain, which was more than I expected. Photos leaked to the local newspaper of Jackson Short at a local gay night club getting frisky with the pool boy. Other photos showed screenshots of him sending lewd and inappropriate text messages to teenage boys. There was no way Vanessa knew any of this; somehow Courtney had dug deep into his personal life, deciding to hold onto these for a rainy day, which happened to be today. A commercial appeared on all the local TV stations, showing a picture of clean cut

Alexander Donner, and a black and white filtered photo of Gordon drinking straight from a bottle of Jack Daniels. "How could a man who has a known adulterer and alcoholic running his campaign have the judgement to make decisions on the city council? Citizens for Accountability approves this message" the commercial said.

The night of the committee meeting came, and I made sure every supporter who showed up had a **Skip! 2018** sign and tee shirt on. Donner showed up, still smiling but without Gordon. Dwayne was also there, but refused to stand anywhere near me. As the candidates were each given two minutes to outline their plans for city council, Skip spoke about policy while Donner spoke about how he fired Gordon like a punk and would allow for more "community input" during the race. The votes from voting committee members were collected and counted. Skip Miller earned 127 votes, and Alexander Donner, Monday's frontrunner was now Saturday's loser with 13 votes. Donner looked defeated as he stood in a corner of the room while Skip gave his acceptance speech. I walked over and placed my business card in his suit's breast pocket. Dwayne walked over to me and patted me on the back to get my attention.

"Bro, you need the Dream Team to save the day this November?" He said to me smiling. I didn't smile back, I didn't look smug, my face was expressionless as I looked at him.

"I'm sorry, do I know you?"

ACT III

"I am Jesus, whom you are persecuting," he replied. "Now get up and go into the city, and you will be told what you must do."
~ACTS CHAPTER 9, VERSE 6, NIV

CHAPTER 10

The Prison Between the Ears

Geoorge Wallace was always the short kid, and on top of that, he was also the poor kid. When he was still in high school, George was the quarterback for his school's football team despite being only ninety-eight pounds soaking wet. Growing up he had to make up for his height with his relentlessness in the boxing ring and his ruthlessness in politics. George Wallace was a fighter, and as he lay in the hospital bed as doctors operated on him, he realized that the fight of his life had only just begun.

He was responsive, but fading in and out of consciousness, unable to stay awake for long. George closed his eyes and at one point found it difficult to open them back up, as if someone glued them shut. Suddenly his hearing went away, and his mind drifted into darkness. Soon he could see, but he wasn't in the hospital room. He stood in a black, dark void and began to freak out.

"You think they'll do it, Mr. Wallace?" a child's voice behind him said. He quickly turned around and saw a little black girl, dressed in her Sunday church clothes, but covered in blood.

"Think they'll do what?" George asked the little girl.

"Do ya think they'll give you a first class funeral?" she clarified to him. George realized it was one of the little girls who had died in the church bombing all those years ago. He began to breathe heavily and sweat. Was this Hell? He thought so. Suddenly he blinked and before he knew it the little girl disappeared. As soon as he realized she was gone, a muscular, veiny red arm put him in a chokehold. Immediately the smell of smoke began to fill up his lungs. George tried to fight back but he was too weak.

"The chickens have come home to roost!" the loud, demonic voice yelled as fire began to erupt from the ground. "The chickens have come home to roost George Corley Wallace!" The demon laughed as George felt the fire start at his feet and started to move up his legs. He tried to scream but nothing came out, he was utterly powerless.

"George!" A familiar voice yelled, "George you need to open your eyes!" It was Cornelia, shaking him back to consciousness. He opened his eyes back up and tried to move, but he couldn't feel his legs.

"Cornelia, I can't move," he said to her. "Why can't I feel my legs?" She kept on her beauty queen smile, thankful that he didn't drift into some kind of coma, but a single tear cascaded down her cheek, unwilling to say aloud what her and George already knew.

It was November 7th, the day after the 2018 midterm election. Corey Stewart, who had succeeded in winning the summer's primary for the Republican senate nomination, spent the rest of the general election cycle begging for cash, firing a good number of his staff, and dealing with controversy after controversy. One of his closest aides was exposed coordinating a follow-up to 2017's deadly rally in Charlottesville. To put a cherry on top of his dumpster fire of a campaign, one of his staffers put up an obviously forged photo of Senator Tim Kaine as a missionary back in his teenage years, sitting down with Contra troops in Nicaragua. The best part of that entire year for Corey was the night he won the nomination, because friends and supporters alike abandoned him as he tried to become something he was not- a fiery populist with nothing to lose. Corey received around forty-one percent of the vote on election day, bringing the Republican Party in Virginia back a decade's worth of progress.

No one could trust him anymore. Corey tried to make Ed Gillespie into some human trafficker in 2017, he burned bridges by spreading vicious lies about Freitas in the primaries in 2018, and he was so desperate for help he was enlisting people with their own intentions of how the race should be run in order to appeal to disgruntled white voters. In the final weeks in the election, after his goose had been all but cooked, Corey tried to make inroads with the Vietnamese community in Northern Virginia, but his attempts seemed disingenuous at best. It was sad too, because I had friends who worked on the campaign because they needed work, but stayed on with him out of a sense of loyalty to the good man they once knew. Corey was Col. Kurtz in *Apocalypse Now*, which his campaign had now come to resemble. All the good men and women who did work for him felt they had to go down the river too because there were no other options, all the way to the end hoping the nightmare would be over November 6th.

I went for a beer with a dear friend of mine a week after the election was over. She had worked for E.W. Jackson in the Senate primary and was enlisted by Corey for the general election only because she had a hard time finding work elsewhere.

"I'm tired, I'm just so tired," she told me. "Corey is at his heart a good man, but he made some poor decisions, decisions he's gonna have to live with because he thought he could spin it."

"Are you working on another campaign after this?" I asked her.

"No, never again. I'm not going to take the abuse and the punches for a candidate who deserves them. These people don't appreciate the people that prop them up. They just want the title and to say they won."

As for my campaign, Skip won his race for city council, solidly beating the Democrat. At Skip's victory party, only staff, volunteers, friends and family were invited, just the people Skip wanted to celebrate with. However, there was a knock at the door no one was expecting. Skip opened it and his face went from cheerful to bothered. Gordon had shown up with a bottle of wine.

"No," I said to Gordon while walking over to the door, "we don't want shit like you here on our night." Gordon looked like trash, trading in his expensive suit for a tracksuit, as well as an unkempt and unbecoming beard he had grown out.

"I know," Gordon said. "I'm not here to bother you, but I just wanted to come and give you this to congratulate you on your victory," he said, passing Skip the bottle. "I'm here to say I'm sorry. I'm sorry for a lot of things. I deserve the way you feel about me, and I can't change that. All I can do is try and be a different man today and tomorrow than I was yesterday. I hope you'll all forgive me, but I don't expect you to." Skip took a step towards Gordon and gave him a hug, it looked like an old father embracing a prodigal son, but I wasn't buying it.

"No, I've trusted you over and over again, and I know you'll never change who you are. I want you to leave, now," I said sternly, concerning the crowd of party guests in the house as they peeked over to see what was going on.

"Art, Gordon is here seeking forgiveness and the Lord wants us to forgive those who seek it," Skip said to me, but I didn't buy it.

"God made the Devil, and I'm seeing an obvious human mistake standing right here," I walked over and punched Gordon, forcing him to fall back out the door. Skip and everyone else was horrified by my act of violence. "You wanna do the world a favor? Just drink yourself to death and leave your body in a dump so no one has to bother figuring out what to do with it."

"Art," Skip said, putting both his hands on my shoulders, "you need to take this back and calm down right now." I looked Skip straight in the eyes and then back to Gordon as he picked himself up and started walking back.

"I think I'm the only honest person Gordon Pecker has ever met in his life," I said to Skip. Gordon drove off and his car disappeared into the distance; this was the last time I ever saw him. I managed to kill the entire vibe of the party. This was supposed to be a day of celebration, but I managed to make it all about myself. Skip wasn't another lying politician; he was a genuinely good man who wanted to serve his community. Something about his embrace and forgiveness of Gordon sickened me though, and I couldn't tell if that said more about him or less about me. There was nothing Skip could have gained by forgiving a broken man, and in my mind that made no sense at all, like a lion defending a lamb. What was the cost of winning if I lost myself in the process? Everything.

Two months later, information leaked out from the Congressman's office that he had developed terminal cancer. The Congressman had intended on making the announcement himself, but according to the expose at Politico, a "disgruntled former staffer, upset with working conditions and the Congressman's deteriorating mind," decided it was best to leak it himself. I found it ironic that Malin was fired the day before the article was published. I think he was blackmailing the Congressman to have more leverage over legislative decisions, but we'll never know. Malin disappeared off the map and the Congressman left Virginia to spend out his remaining days with family in North Carolina. Courtney Cole ran for his seat in a special election, and is now the newest Republican congresswoman from the district. It's strange to know that the most gangster politician I ever personally encountered, the same one who manhandled me for a kiss in a parking lot, was now making decisions that could impact the entire nation. Honestly, she was suited for the job; I even voted for her again.

Vanessa and I spoke a few times after she went to stay with Sabrina's family for about a week after the incident with Jackson. She wrote me a letter in February of 2019 saying she would always love me, but now she needed to move on and learn what it was to love herself, and that I, along with a long list of people that once circled her life, couldn't be part of that. She got rid of all her social media and moved off to Spain. I heard her family opened up a winery there and she got married and had a few kids of her own, finally receiving the love and stability she always deserved.

Jackson moved to Mexico and tried to use his charm and money to buy off an entire town. The local drug cartel didn't appreciate some flamboyant American trying to buy influence on their turf; they saw it as a disrespect. One day Jackson got a package on his mansion's front door, and when he opened it saw the severed head of his former pool boy lover. He then moved back to Virginia into his family's estate, refusing to ever leave the walls of safety and comfort again. His father didn't run for re-election as mayor of their town, meaning the Short political machine finally came to an end.

Dwayne and I never spoke to each other after the local Republican committee meeting. Sabrina bumped into a former campaign colleauge of ours one afternoon while we were out grabbing lunch. She told us Dwayne was fired from multiple jobs after leaving the Congressman's office but was hired to work in fundraising for the Beto O'Rourke presidential campaign.

"So Dwayne's a Democrat now?" Sabrina asked.

"He has always been whatever he needed to be," she replied.

A week after the city council election, Skip and I met with my accountant friend Brent. We had a ton of money left over from the race on account of Courtney's "fuck you" check and other donations, and we had to figure out what to do with it.

"This would help you in your re-election war chest Skip, or you pocket it or donate it, whatever you choose," Brent said while Skip took a sip from his cup of coffee.

"Give it to Art; he's a good kid and I'm not running for re-election, the city needs fresh blood pumping through it to grow regularly," Skip said. Brent and I were stunned; this man was a political anomaly.

"Skip, you don't have to..." I said but he cut me off.

"It comes with conditions though," he said, "you need to go on vacation for a week or so and really consider whether politics is what you want to make your life out of. You've done so much for so many people, but you need to know when it's time to stop before you start making decisions you don't want to make." I paused as I thought about his offer.

"Fine, I agree." Brent filled out the paperwork depositing the remaining campaign funds into my checking account. For the first time in a while, I could take a real vacation. Instead, I used it for the one thing that was far from the first idea on my mind- therapy.

I started attending an Alcoholics Anonymous group at the local Catholic Church on my street. Before I started going to meetings, I had already been sober for two months, but I appreciated the continued support. No alcohol meant no strange apparitions or hallucinations. I also started seeing a therapist regularly, someone to help me figure out my anger and depression so I could put it in front of me in an objective environment and actually make some personal progress. So much about campaigns and politics is about spinning the news, turning lies into truths, and justifying bad actions with good results. It was so difficult for me to piece together what was going on inside my head, but I was getting there one day at a time.

"So this Satan figure looked like Richard Nixon?" she asked me.

"Yeah, I know it's weird," I replied as she was jotting down notes on her notepad.

"Why Nixon?" she asked.

"I guess because my parents always hated him or something like that or whatever."

"You think you project Richard Nixon and Satan together as one person because he embodies the negative side of your personality? A manifestation of bad actions and guilt?" she asked.

I was taken aback. It was really weird hearing someone say that out loud.

"When I was on vacation in Las Vegas with my girlfriend after my last campaign, I only had the intention of drinking one shot of vodka, but then I had another, and another until I lost count. I was expecting he'd jump over my shoulder and call me a loser and a liar, but he didn't. All I saw as I looked down into the tiny bottom of the glass was my own reflection. I'm the only one who chooses to make my own decisions, no one else and that is what bothers me down to my core," I said.

"That clarifies it Art; Satan Nixon is a dark reflection of you," she replied. I paused for a moment, trying to just soak everything in without getting emotional. "Everyone has a Satan Nixon on their shoulder, sometimes they overshadow the angel that's supposed to be on the other shoulder because, ultimately, we are good people who want to do good things, despite our natural flaws and fall from grace. They don't lie to us either, that is the difficult part we have to understand. They tell us the truths we want to hear, and that is why they're so seductive. We sometimes conceptualize them into something we hate because we don't want to admit what we are doing is our decision."

"This is a lot for me to process, doctor," I said.

"You're in politics so you should know, why do people hate Hillary Clinton so much? Or Donald Trump? I mean we all know the people who hate them and consider them the most evil beings in the world, but they also don't know their other names." I was confused.

"What other names?" I asked.

"Someone calls her 'mom' and others call him 'dad'" she said. "They don't see them as human; they see them as their greatest fears and insecurities. They can't just be people we see on the TV often; they have to become an excuse for our misfortunes and our anger. We pin many of our problems on them and others because we don't want to confront the problems within ourselves. Besides, if we can't forgive those who hurt us, how can we ever expect others to forgive us when we make a mistake we can't truly make amends for?"

News of Wallace being gunned down travelled from coast to coast immediately. It took the country by storm as a second presidential candidate in four years was shot at a rally. For many, however, they didn't know what to do as they found out the victim was George Wallace. Did they pray? Did they laugh? Depending on who you spoke to you got different answers. However, the question on everyone's mind was how on earth George Wallace survived, whereas both Kennedys and MLK didn't. Some folks have asked themselves what type of God would let George Wallace live, and let those other men die.

In California, one governor's press conference was interrupted by the news of the Wallace shooting. Governor Ronald Reagan, a former Hollywood star, Republican young gun, and at the time Governor of California, was interrupted during the middle of a press conference by his press secretary alerting him that Governor Wallace had just been shot, and no one knew whether he was dead or alive.

"Oh no, this is a news bulletin that I'm sure will be of great interest to every one of you," Reagan said to get the attention of the reporters who were getting ready to leave as the conference wrapped up. "It's just been passed down to me by my press secretary the AP and the UPI report that Governor George Wallace has been shot during an appearance in Laurel, Maryland, and he was taken to a hospital by ambulance. There are no further details as of yet." The reporters immediately ran to any available phones, radios, and televisions to see if they could get any word on what just happened. However, Reagan had just enough of them still standing in the room to occupy their attention for at least one more moment before he'd lose them entirely.

"Well that gives me a chance, and I don't suppose there's any questions anymore about any questions," the Governor continued, "but isn't this again something that we've been talking about? We've had so many tragedies over the last several years in the area of political candidates and office holders of this kind and isn't this an outgrowth of the hatred of what seems to be injected, what has been in the past has been normal competition and normal rivalry, and certainly election year emotionalism and all, but if something is to be done about this kind of tragedy for anyone, isn't it necessary that all of us review our own attitude and say yes, it is possible for men and women of good will to differ to have opposing viewpoints to discuss and debate them, and perhaps never come to agreement on them but, as God as in his Heaven, do we have to hate each other to the point where people with less balance are stimulated to deeds of this kind?"

Wallace recovered and several weeks later was discharged from the hospital, completely paralyzed from the waist down but still willing to resume regular campaign activities. In many ways, most voters respected the tenacity of Wallace willing to take a tragedy and instead focus on his policies of trade reform, a strong military, and fighting big government. However by the time he was released, the Florida

Democratic Convention was already underway and George McGovern was now the presumptive Democratic nominee. The DNC, as a show of good faith to the loyal Wallace voting bloc, allowed Wallace to address the convention. As he was rolled onto the stage in his wheelchair, the crowd stood and gave him a roaring applause. However, as he began to speak, he was largely ignored.

In addressing the convention, he aimed to remind the Democrats that he wished for the party to go back to being the party of working people, not social justice. That big government liberalism would impede on the freedoms of everyday normal people and without a respect for law enforcement and the military, our image abroad would be seen as weakness by our enemies. His words fell flat on the ears of those in attendance, and his days as the fiery George Wallace were now behind.

Something changed in George after the campaign ended. He was quieter and didn't want to be seen in public as often. Cornelia tried what she could to get him out of the house, but his spirit was as broken as his hope of getting to walk again. In an interview around 1997, she commented that after he was released from the hospital, she vowed never to let him see her in a state of self-pity or shed a tear ever again. Cornelia reflected on what she missed about George after the assassination attempt, telling the reporter she missed that "feisty walk of his" and it broke her that she'd never see it again.

While still recovering and attending physical therapy, Wallace still had a state to run. He appointed trusted people whom he knew could work without his supervision, but there were still some things that only the governor could do, those being ceremonial duties. In 1973, at the University of Alabama homecoming game, Terry Points Boney made history by being elected by her peers to become the first black homecoming queen in Alabama history. Wallace was there on stage with her, as she leaned down to make it easier for Wallace to crown her. He said his congratulations, even commenting on how beautiful she was, and the two went their separate ways as the game was about to begin. To have the first black homecoming queen crowned by the most controversial former segregationist in the country was a shot heard around the world. Years later, people would ask Boney of her interaction with Wallace. "He was as I would expect the governor to be: cordial," she'd reply.

While Wallace seemed cheerful in public, his personal life came crashing down around him. For years after the shooting, his marriage with Cornelia began to take a toll and his health was only getting worse. In 1976, Wallace attempted his final bid for the Democratic nomination, but was undercut by another southern governor who was gaining popularity, Jimmy Carter. Wallace lost the Florida primary to Carter, the same state which he carried every county in back in 1972. The press wouldn't let up, constantly taking photos of him being lifted from his wheelchair into his car. The straw that broke the camel's back was when a staffer dropped Wallace while carrying him into a plane, injuring his already immobile right leg. Wallace had enough of the circus and dropped out of the race right before endorsing Jimmy Carter.

In 1978, George and Cornelia ended their marriage in a heavily publicized and bloody divorce. For years Cornelia had suspected George had been cheating on her with other women, so she decided to tap the phones in the Governor's Mansion. Not only did she discover he was having lewd conversations behind her back with younger women, but George had also been spreading rumors that she was having an affair with a state trooper. The years she had nursed him back from the peak of death had taken a toll on her, and this break in trust was enough for her to finally confront George. Angered, she tapped his phone calls, and he initiated the divorce. After they divorced, Cornelia received no alimony and became a taboo discussion topic throughout Alabama. Cornelia moved back to Florida to be close to her sons, while George stayed in the mansion alone, with nothing but his thoughts.

One night while George slept alone in his bed, he dreamt of a time when he could walk. He was back home with his wife and children. Lurleen was preparing dinner while the daughters were playing. He heard George Jr. practicing his guitar in his room.

"You're getting good with that," George said to his fourteen-year-old son. "How about you play me a song you learned?" George Jr. had just learned how to play and sing Bob Dylan's "The Times They Are A-Changin'." George was proud watching his son play so well, but a certain verse stuck in like a knife as he continued listening.

"Come senators, congressmen, please heed the call. Don't stand in the doorway, don't block up the hall..." George Jr. sang. George looked him straight in the eyes, startled down to his core. This wasn't just a random song; Bob Dylan was talking directly to the symbol of opposition — him. George woke up, back in his broken body all alone in his mansion. What type of man was he? What other terrible things in his life were the result of something he said or did, or refused to do? He grabbed a Bible on his nightstand and began reading. He wouldn't leave the mansion for days.

During that time George did write out a letter to a man incarcerated in Maryland. The letter was to Arthur Bremer, who was now twenty-eight years old and serving his sentence for attempted murder. Bremer failed to achieve what he wanted, not necessarily the assassination, but the love and affection his poisoned mind had convinced him he'd earned. Wardens described Bremer as a model prisoner, but also noted he was a loner, completely solitary compared to the other inmates. George had something to say to Bremer; in his letter he told him that he loved him as a brother and child of God, and that he forgave him for what he did. The letter emphasized that if Bremer would ask forgiveness from the Lord and accept Christ Jesus into his heart, than maybe one day, they'd be in Heaven together. This wasn't a one-off moment for Wallace; he understood that if he couldn't forgive Bremer for the pain he had inflicted on his life, what were the odds that God would forgive him for his sins?

Bremer was just the start for Wallace's road to Damascus. His first call out of the series of calls he made to all those he had wronged in his life was to a city councilman from Atlanta, Georgia, and a civil rights activist who had been brutally assaulted during the 1965 police riot in Selma. Councilman John Lewis picked up the phone, and for a moment was suspended in disbelief as the man he least expected to ever call was on the other line, crying his heart out.

"I don't hate anyone, John. I don't hate anyone," Wallace pleaded. After a long conversation, Lewis forgave Wallace for the sins of his past and the hurt he had inflicted on him but made it clear that words without action were no different than lies.

Remso W. Martinez

CHAPTER 11

Brother George

I was asleep when Colin called me. I wanted the call just to go to voicemail so I could call him in the morning, but I knew something wasn't right. I hadn't spoken to Colin in over a year now and for him to call me so late at night instead of just sending me a text was out of the norm. The call went to voicemail, but he immediately called again. This was something important.

"Art," he said as I clicked answer, "he's dead man, Gordon Pecker is dead." I laid back in bed as Colin told me what went down. I just stared at the ceiling without a single solitary thought going through my mind. I wasn't sad, I wasn't confused, I sure wasn't happy. I was just in a state of pure shock, and it took me days until I'd feel an ounce of anything.

Gordon had started going back to his Alcoholics Anonymous meetings. From what Colin had heard he was making some real progress, and his wife let him move back into the house so they could work on their marriage. One afternoon while Gordon and his wife Lisa took the kids out to the park, there was a child who was ignored by his father while the dad was busy focusing on his cell phone. Gordon felt something was wrong so he kept an eye on the kid who was setting up a kite. Everything was okay, but a few minutes later, the kid tossed the kite into the air to catch a gust of wind. The boy was running and running as if he had just done the coolest thing imaginable while the father still focused on his cell phone. Gordon was paying attention however, and immediately ran to the boy the moment he realized what no one else had.

The boy was running towards the road where a large semi-truck was approaching, with no sign of slowing down. The kid wasn't paying attention to anything other than his kite. Within a few seconds of stepping foot on the road, Gordon had been able to sprint over there and push the boy away from the semi. What took everyone else's attention from what they had previously been doing was the large splat they heard hit the road. The boy looked back and let go of his kite, caught up in the wind as he looked back to see what had happened to the man who saved him. The kite dangled in the air, dipping downwards before being picked up once again, only to fly higher and farther away until it was lost in the distance.

A week later was his funeral, and only a few friends he made in his AA group and family were in attendance. Skip showed up too, and I did mainly because he had asked me to. He realized I was feeling guilty over our last encounter where I punched Gordon and said he'd be better off dead. Skip was right; I'm still glad I listened to him. As we went to the cemetery   and him into his final resting place, his wife Lisa walked up to me as I pulled out a flask from my jacket and contemplated an innocent swig.

"I'm sorry, but I don't remember ever meeting you," she said as I put the flask back in my jacket. "Did you know my husband?" she asked as I looked past her shoulder to the newly placed tombstone that was Gordon's grave.

"No," I replied, "I didn't really know your husband too well." We spoke for another minute and went our separate ways. Driving home, it had rained lightly, but off to the side of the country road I saw a yellow kite without an owner gliding on its own in the distance. A moment later it disappeared into the horizon. I lowered my driver's side window, reached into my suit pocket, tossed the flask out the window and watched it skid on the empty road behind me as it disappeared into the distance.

I pulled over to a McDonald's on the side of the highway on my long drive back to Fairfax. Max Getty sent me a text message with a link to a story saying Corey Stewart had quit politics for good. "Politics sucks. On a personal level, it's been a disaster," Stewart told *the Washington Post*, discussing the toll it took on his health, his family, and his law practice which lost half its revenue in a year. I understood where he was coming from, I really did, and for a moment I felt bad for him. I believe that was the most honest statement to come out of Corey's mouth in a long time, and for that I pitied him and said a prayer in the McDonald's parking lot, hoping he'd focus on living a good life and being the provider his wife and sons needed him to be.

When I got back into town, I met up with Max. We spoke about the new Super PAC he started around the time of the Brett Kavanaugh Supreme Court hearings. He also said he was taking advantage of the black-face scandal that hit the Virginia Governor's and Attorney General's office to shine a light on some up and coming candidates he was grooming, pushing them in front of as many cameras as possible to scream racism and to demand resignations. We spoke about his ultimate plans for 2020, which were to go to the frontlines of every battlefield state in the nation and unload his war chest in the President's honor so we could keep America great.

"You're a smart and talented guy Art. Come make some money with me and let's have some fun this cycle," Max said. For a moment the offer was tempting, but I looked behind the bar table we were sitting at and looked at the two TV's that were on, set to two competing news networks: one calling one half of America deplorable and the other station calling the other half ungodly.

"I'm gonna try out a career change, go take a bottle of wine to Virginia Beach for a few more days so I can dip my feet in the sand and think about a few things." Max knew exactly what I was saying, but I just couldn't say the words. He leaned in for a hug, like a master saying goodbye to his student.

"I know what you're saying kid, I know."

"Who's the white man in the wheelchair sitting in the back of service?" A young black teenager pointed and asked his mother as their Sunday service at the local Baptist church began to wrap up. She quickly slapped his hand.

"Don't you point at that man," she said sternly to her child. "That's Governor Wallace, and he's our guest today." Every Sunday and even on some Wednesdays, George attended many different church services at predominantly black churches throughout the state. This was him, taking in the word of God while using what little time he had left on Earth to talk about his life, his regrets, and to ask each congregation for their forgiveness. Like a prodigal son, he was embraced, and a part of him that hadn't felt alive in decades began to come through for the rest of the world to see as this man of broken body, but healed heart spilled his soul to those that had every right to hate the man he was, and ignore the old, broken man before them.

"George Wallace is a child of God," one member of one of the many Baptist churches Wallace had visited said. "God said you must repent, and he repented," she said with tears of joy in her eyes, "this is a new George Wallace and a child of God, and you can believe that."

While his relationship with God was starting a new chapter, his relationship with Cornelia would come to a heartbreaking end. On several occasions after their divorce over the next few years, he would ask her over the phone to move back to Alabama and marry him again, but her sons protested, reminding her of why they divorced in the first place.

In 1981, George Wallace married Lisa Taylor, who was only thirty-two years of age when she married the sixty-one-year-old Wallace. Taylor, when still a teenager, wrote the theme song for Wallace's 1968 presidential campaign, and like Cornelia, was also a country singer. Cornelia spoke to press back in Alabama, saying the marriage was a joke, and the buxom young blonde was taking advantage of the old man. "I have not given up hope of a reconciliation. I made a commitment to be a wife, and that's what I really want to be."

In 1982, Wallace made his final run for Governor of Alabama and won ninety percent of the black vote. He dedicated the remainder of his political career to what he always intended to: serving the poor and the ignored, the same environment that Wallace, as a child watching his grandfather in Clio help the lame and sick in exchange for eggs and jams, had come from. By 1984 during the Democratic primaries for president, many candidates would come to Alabama to seek the wisdom and possible endorsement of the old Governor. One of the most memorable was the first black candidate for president, Jesse Jackson. Wallace's advice to Jackson was comical in a way, telling him "always listen to your security."

In 1986, Wallace realized his time in the ring was over, and the best decision would be to retire from the public eye while he still had his full mental capacities. In his farewell address to the Alabama state legislature, Wallace said his goodbyes. "I would like to be part of the future myself, but in the last few days, I have done much evaluation and much searching, and some of you who are younger may not realize but I paid a pretty high price in 1972. Those five bullets gave me a thorn in the flesh...I realized that my own mind, while I'm doing very good at the present time, as I grow older the effects of my problem might be more noticeable. I feel that I must say I've climbed my last political mountain, but there are still some personal hills that I must climb. But for now I must pass the rope and the pick to another climber and say climb on, climb on to higher heights. Climb on till you reach the very peak, then look back and wave at me, I too will still be climbing. My fellow Alabamans, I bid you a fond and passionate farewell."

Wallace would divorce Taylor in 1987, and never reconciled with Cornelia for the remainder of his life. Before Cornelia passed away a decade and a half later, she said one of her greatest regrets was not getting back together with George.

George C. Wallace died from an infection linked to the 1972 assassination attempt in 1997. In 2007, Arthur Bremer was released from prison. According to a Maryland Corrections official, "Arthur Bremer is alone, he has no one." Cornelia Wallace, who never remarried, died in 2009 from cancer.

George Wallace Jr. would go on to serve in Alabama politics as well and has since become an outspoken conservative. In talks with the press over the years regarding his father's legacy, he said his father's most proud accomplishment had nothing to do with his success in politics; it had everything to do with his love and faith in God.

CHAPTER 12

Damascus

In the book of Acts, chapter nine, the Roman persecutor of Christians, Saul, was struck down by God and blinded before accepting Jesus Christ. As a result of his conversion, Saul changed his name to Paul and went on to establish thousands of Churches so he could save as many souls as possible. He didn't have a car, GPS, campaign manager or a giant fundraising machine; Paul traveled on foot and talked to people. Paul, who had the rights of Romans and a life of privilege, left it all behind to become a martyr for Jesus.

My faith has been tested many times, but Paul's story is what convinces me the Bible is real. The dude left his cushy life behind and became a traveling homeless guy that got beat up and bitten by snakes on a regular basis, but never let his faith waver. Six months after Gordon died, I became a journalist and a columnist for a local paper. I felt better covering real news and focusing on people who needed it instead of serving myself and some opportunist with a campaign slogan. Colin and I had been chatting quite a bit and decided on one afternoon to get some dinner.

"Do you still have the money that Skip gave you or did you spend it all?" Colin asked.

"Believe it or not, I didn't spend any of it. Part of me just doesn't want to," I replied. Colin had an idea, something we could actually do that could use money tainted by malice and repurpose it for good. We gave a third of it to Lisa Pecker so she didn't have to worry about saving for college for her children. The remainder of it was used to start a charity for children in lower income communities so we could provide them with school supplies and books. Colin called it the Gordon Pecker Memorial Fund, a tribute to a man whose life was defined by one solitary action, showing us that those who we give up on are still capable of being good.

We went out to get lunch again one afternoon after officially setting up the fund with the bank and getting to bring a check to each of the local schools. Beto O'Rourke was on TV, probably the last person Colin, a strident Republican originally from Texas, wanted to see.

"God, that man is the freaking Devil," Colin said. I stopped eating and looked directly at him.

"I think we overuse calling people the Devil, Colin," I said back.

"You're right, I just think he's stupid," he replied.

"That's better," I said as we both started laughing.

Later that day I got back home and saw Sabrina, sitting in a kitchen chair looking back at me, all smiles.

"What are you happy about?" I asked her. She pulled out a box from behind her with test tubes and swabs. "Sabrina, tell me you didn't order that Ancestry DNA thing so you can swab me."

"Nope," she said with a giggle, "I already swabbed your cheek while you slept weeks ago." I started laughing as I walked around the table to see the results on her laptop.

"If it says I'm related to Fidel Castro, we're never talking about this, ever," I said. She was scrolling through the family tree as results were loading. We focused on my mother's side of the family, and a few minutes in we stopped and just looked blankly at the laptop screen. One of the family tree branches showed me a connection which made us both pause, wipe our eyes, and refresh the page a few times.

"Well..." Sabrina said with a lingering pause, "Say hello to your cousin George."

NOTES

FACT VS FICTION: RETELLING THE LIFE OF GEORGE WALLACE

Numerous sources were consulted in order to craft an accurate narrative telling of the real life of George Wallace, but the primary sources that were used to write the book are provided here.

GETTING THE DIALOGUE RIGHT

Almost all of the dialogue between the characters in the George Wallace arc of the story was taken from the *American Experience* documentary series by historian David McCullough. This was the best source for accuracy since the series utilized both archival footage and eyewitness testimonies in order to provide the most accurate and objective telling of the life of George Wallace. To this day, this series has still proven to be the most complete source for information on Wallace despite the multiple films and unauthorized biographies that have come about since his death in 1998.

McCullough, David, director. *American Experience Presents: George Wallace: Settin' the Woods on Fire. American Experience*, PBS, 2000, www.tvguide.com/tvshows/american-experience/episode-13-season-12/george-wallace-settin-the-woods-on-fire/191373/.

Additional dialogue specific to the 1968 presidential campaign cycle as well as the overall description of that contentious period in American history was taken from the three-part *Ball of Confusion* docuseries produced by the University of Virginia Center for Politics. The story of *the New York Times* reporter and his son's encounter with Wallace was reported by *The Christian Science Monitor*.

Sabato, Larry, director. *Ball of Confusion. YouTube*, University of Virginia Center for Politics, 1 Mar. 2016, www.youtube.com/watch?v=yWmRZUnFXtc.

Monitor, The Christian Science, director. *George Wallace: Donald Trump's Predecessor in Attacking the Media. YouTube*, YouTube, 7 Aug. 2018, www.youtube.com/watch?v=YMQnMbRGhLE.

CORNELIA WALLACE

Additional information that was specific to the life of Cornelia Wallace.

Windham, Ben. "SOUTHERN LIGHTS: Courageous Cornelia Had, Then Lost, It All." *www.tuscaloosanews.com*, 18 Jan. 2009, www.tuscaloosanews.com/news/20090118/southern-lights-courageous-cornelia-had-then-lost-it-all.

ASA CARTER

The introduction to Asa Carter in Chapter 6 is a completely fictitious re-telling of Carter's introduction to Wallace. Seymour Trammell never knew Carter nor introduced him to Wallace. Creative liberties were taken for this scene in order to move the story along. According to some accounts, Carter was a fan of Wallace and pursued him after attending one of his speeches in order to solicit a job as a speechwriter for his second campaign for the governorship. Much of Carter's life is unknown; he also went by the name "Forrest Carter" in order to create a new identity for himself after his failed campaign for governor. Carter would go on to write several widely popular novels such as "The Rebel Outlaw: Josie Wales" and "The Education of Little Tree."

Ricci, Marco, director. *The Reconstruction of Asa Carter. ITVS*, IMDb.com, 2012, www.imdb.com/title/tt1540120/.

WALLACE AND LBJ

Creative liberties were taken in order to write the scene in which Wallace spoke to President Johnson in the Oval Office. There are no credible accounts of what the two men specifically said to each other, only conflicting stories that have become myths over time. The facts that are known are that President Johnson did host Governor Wallace in the White House for a meeting in the Oval Office and the topic of voting rights for African-Americans was discussed. The dialogue used to craft this specific part in the story was inspired by the films *George Wallace* (1997) and *Selma* (2014) which both showed this scene with varying degrees of difference.

Frankenheimer, John, director. *George Wallace*. IMDb, Turner Network Television, 1997, www.imdb.com/title/tt0119189/.

DuVernay, Ava, director. *Selma*. IMDb, Harpo Films, 2014, www.imdb.com/title/tt1020072/.

WALLACE ON *FIRING LINE* WITH WILLIAM F. BUCKLEY JR.

De Caprio, Al, director. *Firing Line: The Wallace Crusade*. IMDb, IMDb.com, 24 Jan. 1968, www.imdb.com/title/tt4056086/.

HUNTER S. THOMPSON ON WALLACE

Lott, Jeremy. *Fear and Loathing and Wallace and Cruz*, Washington Examiner, 6 Apr. 2016, www.washingtonexaminer.com/fear-and-loathing-and-wallace-and-cruz

Thompson, Hunter S. *Fear and Loathing: on the Campaign Trail '72*. Simon & Schuster Paperbacks, 2012.

RONALD REAGAN SPEECH AND WALLACE'S NIGHTMARE

The nightmare sequence described in Chapter 10 is fiction. It was written into the story in order to convey the turning point in Wallace's life where he lived out the rest of his days not only in a wheelchair, but also seeking forgiveness for his past mistakes. The audio clip of (then) Governor Ronald Reagan's reaction to the Wallace assassination attempt is provided in the link below.

https://www.youtube.com/watch?v=aH3Yz9mBqdU

THE BOB DYLAN DREAM

Creative liberties were taken in crafting the scene that was the basis of the dream sequence in Chapter 10. The true story was recounted by George Wallace Jr. to *Tuscaloosa News* in 2012, in which he talked about a time during his teenage years when his father asked him to play for him a song he learned on the guitar, which happened to be Bob Dylan's song "The Times They Are A Changin'." The look of obvious shock and guilt expressed by Wallace as told by Wallace Jr. was what inspired the writing of this specific portion of the story.

Grayson, Wayne. "Son Says Former Gov. George Wallace Repented for Past." *www.tuscaloosanews.com,* 8 June 2012, www.tuscaloosanews.com/article/DA/20120608/News/605152896/TL/ .

WALLACE CROWNS THE HOMECOMING QUEEN

Johnson, Roy. "Alabama's First African-American Homecoming Queen Attributes It to 'the Time and Timing,' Reflects on Meeting George Wallace." *Al.com,* 5 Oct. 2016, www.al.com/news/birmingham/2016/10/alabams_first_african-american.html.

SOURCES IN REFERENCE TO MENTIONS OF COREY STEWART

Cleary, Ronica. "Trump's Va. Campaign Chair Corey Stewart Fired for Organizing Protest Outside RNC." *Http://www.fox5dc.Com*, 10 Oct. 2016, www.fox5dc.com/news/trump-va-state-chairmans-job-is-in-jeopardy.

Koma, Alex. "Corey Stewart's Insults of Ed Gillespie Prompt Republican Condemnations." *www.insidenova.com*, 24 Mar. 2017, www.insidenova.com/headlines/corey-stewart-s-insults-of-ed-gillespie-prompt-republican-condemnations/article_eeee64d6-10cf-11e7-ba0d-a3997a46f12f.html.

Vozzella, Laura. "Stewart Calls Gillespie's Work for Tyson Foods 'Human Trafficking'." *www.newsleader.com*, 31 May 2017, www.newsleader.com/story/news/local/2017/05/31/stewart-calls-gillespies-work-tyson-foods-human-trafficking/357714001/

Moomaw, Graham. "Corey Stewart, Toilet Paper in Hand Outside State Capitol, Takes Swipes at Republicans Who Support Medicaid Expansion." *www.roanoke.com*, 22 Feb. 2018, www.roanoke.com/news/politics/general_assembly/corey-stewart-toilet-paper-in-hand-outside-state-capitol-takes/article_d7d54a94-d884-5d74-8dbd-41c41e4956c5.html.

Wilson, Patrick. "GOP's Nick Freitas Says at Liberty University Debate That Corey Stewart's Camp Attacked His Ethnicity." *www.richmond.com*, 19 Apr. 2018, www.richmond.com/news/virginia/government-politics/gop-s-nick-freitas-says-at-liberty-university-debate-that/article_44c592e9-01ab-5940-aba5-3a8ef476664a.html.

Dickinson, Tim. "Virginia Republicans Are Rallying Behind a True Bigot: Corey Stewart." *www.rollingstone.com*, 13 June 2018, www.rollingstone.com/politics/politics-news/virginia-republicans-are-rallying-behind-a-true-bigot-corey-stewart-628439/.

Weill, Kelly. "GOP Candidate Corey Stewart's Spokesperson Called Majority-Black Cities 'Shitholes.'" *www.dailybeast.com*, 30 July 2018, www.thedailybeast.com/gop-candidate-corey-stewarts-spokesperson-called-majority-black-cities-shitholes.

Hakim, Danny. "White Nationalists Love Corey Stewart. He Keeps Them Close." *www.nytimes.com*, 5 Aug. 2018, www.nytimes.com/2018/08/05/us/politics/corey-stewart-virginia.html.

Olivo, Antonio, and Patricia Sullivan. "Corey Stewart, the Firebrand Virginia Republican, Will Leave Politics in December ." *www.washingtonpost.com*, 8 Jan. 2019, www.washingtonpost.com/local/virginia-politics/corey-stewart-the-firebrand-virginia-republican-will-leave-politics-in-december/2018/12/27/71f08a3c-04b0-11e9-9122-82e98f91ee6f_story.html?noredirect=on&utm_term=.0127b68cc14b.

THE VICE NEWS INTERVIEW

Pelosi, Alexandra, director. *Don't Get Rolled | Goodbye, Congress: A VICE News Tonight Special Report. YouTube*, Vice News, 3 Jan. 2019, www.youtube.com/watch?v=YlGwqUBvuqM.

ACKNOWLEDGMENTS

I want to thank my team of editors Logan Albright, Cassie Bowns, and Emily Sebast for working so diligently to ensure readers had the best experience possible reading through the book. I want to thank my publicist Chloe Anagnos for assisting me in making sure the marketing of this book was as effective and seamless as possible.

I want to thank everyone who helped me exceed my Indiegogo campaign goal of raising $1,000 for production costs to make this book into a reality. Without you, this book would not be in the fantastic form it is. A big, special thank you to everyone that went above and beyond to ensure this dream turned into a reality including William Alonso, Tyler Colford, William Wells, Mike Feuz, Sean Valerga, Victoria Morrical, Krysti Avery, Anthony Welti, Joel Davis, Jay Caetano, Quest Fanning, Lee LeTourneau, Dan Smotz, Ryan Lindsey, Sean Doyle, Raylene Lightheart, Kaytee Moyer, Tina Freitas, Al Billingsly, Kristopher Evans, Craig de Costa, Flanna Sheridan, Brian Soujanen, Eli Bowman, Mary Jo Pilkinton, and Matt Augustine.

ABOUT THE AUTHOR

Remso W. Martinez is an author and journalist from Virginia. You can learn more about him by visiting his website rwmartinez.com.

70876016R00099

Made in the USA
Middletown, DE
28 September 2019